Back Room Girl

Back Room Girl

Donna Baker

Thorndike Press • Chivers Press
Thorndike, Maine USA   Bath, England

This Large Print edition is published by Thorndike Press, USA and by Chivers Press, England.

Published in 1999 in the U.S. by arrangement with Chivers Press Limited.

Published in 1999 in the U.K. by arrangement with Severn House Publishers Ltd.

U.S. Hardcover 0-7862-2261-1 (Romance Series Edition)
U.K. Hardcover 0-7540-1375-8 (Windsor Large Print)
U.K. Softcover 0-7540-2280-3 (Paragon Large Print)

The text of this Large Print edition is unabridged.
Other aspects of the book may vary from the original edition.

Set in 16 pt. Plantin.

Printed in the United States on permanent paper.

British Library Cataloguing-in-Publication Data available

Library of Congress Cataloging-in-Publication Data

Baker, Donna.
    Back room girl / Donna Baker.
        p.   cm.
    ISBN 0-7862-2261-1 (lg. print : hc : alk. paper)
    1. Large type books. I. Title.
PR6052.A327 B33   1999
    823′.914—dc21   99-046979

Back Room Girl

One

It went almost without saying, Rachel Grant thought with resignation, that the man already waiting outside the interview room would look at her with astonishment. She'd grown accustomed to that, as she'd worked her way up through what was still so much a man's world. She didn't even mind now; it was a challenge to make that look change to one of respect rather than a mixture of physical admiration and male condescension.

"Yes, I *am* being interviewed for the job," she said without waiting for him to ask. "The same one as you — if you're applying to be Assistant Designer." And she waited patiently while his eyes moved over her rippling cloud of coppery hair, taking in her oval face and sea-green eyes before assessing her slender figure, his expression all the while saying clearer than words what he thought of her chances of landing such a job; or of her even having the qualifications to apply for it in the first place.

"You design cars?" he said at last, and Rachel smiled slightly at the faint outrage in his tone.

"That's right. I've been working with Britton Cars." She felt a small satisfaction as his eyebrows went up. "I worked on the design of the Britton Beagle." There was no need to say more; the respect was there, still tinged with surprise, and behind it was dawning a faint anxiety. Rachel smiled to herself, guessing that her rival had already assumed he would get the job. Now he wasn't so sure — and that meant she'd passed her first test.

As the door opened and her companion was called in to the interview room, Rachel sat back and opened a magazine. Outwardly, she knew she appeared calm and self-possessed; inwardly, her heart was thumping raggedly and her breath was beginning to come more quickly. She took a few slow, deep breaths and felt a little better. Getting nervous now wasn't going to help at all, she told herself. A little apprehension was a good thing — it helped the adrenalin to flow, so that she could give of her best — but more than that was a definite handicap. Especially when you were already handicapped to start with, merely by being a woman.

Getting to the top of her profession as a designer in engineering — and in one of the fields most jealously guarded by men — had been an uphill struggle for Rachel. She'd had to fight every inch of the way, fighting both male and female prejudice, for even now a good many women watched such progress with a jaundiced eye, and fighting even her own good looks, which caused so many men to take a patronising attitude towards her. It hadn't been easy to persuade them that behind her smooth forehead lay a brain that could work as efficiently as any man's, and produce as good designs.

And now, after three years spent with one of the top motor manufacturers of the country, here she was waiting for an interview with a man who had the reputation of being one of the most difficult and exacting employers in the industry. She must be mad, she told herself ruefully, for perhaps the hundredth time. Throwing up a secure and interesting position for — what? But the answer came at once, and with it all her certainty that here was the job she'd hankered for. The chance to work with a highly individual motor manufacturer, whose cars were instantly recognizable and had a worldwide reputation; who had had the strength of mind to resist all the temptations of mass production and continue to produce cars that were virtually handmade, so few of them that they could almost be described as 'limited editions', so desirable that pop stars, Arab sheikhs and even royalty were willing to wait several years for their orders.

Quentin Motors were something special. A relatively small firm, situated near a country town close to the Welsh border — hardly ideal for a competitive industry, Rachel had thought as she drove through winding country lanes with primrose-studded banks. Yet it didn't seem to matter. It probably even enhanced Quentin's reputation for the wayward individuality its cars expressed. She felt that by moving into the industrial Midlands the firm would have lost something, something indefinable, yet essential.

And Lorne Quentin, owner and managing director of the family firm established fifty years ago, was something special too. An enigma, appearing often in the financial pages and occasionally in the gossip columns as he escorted the latest beauty, yet aloof and essentially private, as Rachel had discovered when she'd tried to find out more about him and failed.

Well, she would soon know the worst, — soon know whether Lorne Quentin was a woman-hater, as far as those designing motor-cars went at any rate, or whether he was enlightened enough to keep sex right out of the situation. He might even — she smiled at the thought — be that rarity she'd been looking for: the man who didn't even notice she *was* a woman. Though she had to admit, as she brushed back her mane of glowing auburn hair and glanced down at the pale grey suede suit that enhanced her soft curves, that it would take a peculiarly dedicated man to miss the fact.

Well, perhaps Lorne Quentin *was* that man. She would find out in a very short time now.

It seemed, however, a very long time before the door opened and the other applicant came out. He gave Rachel a glance that was part-rueful, part-complacent, and went off down the corridor. Rachel waited, taking deep breaths, and after a few moments a blond head looked round the door and its owner said pleasantly, "Would you like to come in now, please, Miss Grant?"

Well, *this* wasn't Lorne Quentin, that was for sure, Rachel thought as she stood up

11

and followed the man through the door. She found herself in a small outer office, waiting at another door, and gave her companion a quick, comprehensive glance. A little taller than she, with thick fair hair and a friendly, interested face — no, this wasn't the enigmatic Adonis of the gossip columns. Pity — she had a feeling that she and this affable-looking young man would get along quite well together.

"I'm Mike Dalton," he told her, holding out his hand and giving hers a firm shake. "Lorne's Chief Designer. You'd be working with me, so I'll be sharing the interview." His sudden grin was heart-warming and reassuring, and as she went through the office door behind him Rachel felt much better.

But not for long. One glance at Lorne Quentin's austere face, the black brows lowering over cold grey eyes, the unsmiling mouth above the square jaw, told her that everything she'd heard about this man was true, and then some. Difficult, exacting and, if not hostile, something very close to it. For a brief moment, her heart sank and she wondered if it were even worth continuing with an interview whose outcome seemed all too certain. Then she took herself to task mentally and squared her shoulders. What was she thinking of? She hadn't come this far just to let one glance from cool grey eyes destroy all her efforts, had she? After all her hard work, she wasn't about to let any man, whatever his position, whatever his reputation, swerve her from her ambition.

An ambition that had brought her close to the top of the ladder. An ambition that wouldn't let her rest until she was right there on the highest rung, looking down on a host of competitors who were mostly male.

Only Lorne Quentin stood between her and the next rung, which wasn't the top one itself, but was dizzyingly close. It was up to her to see that he didn't block her way however prejudiced he might be.

Lorne Quentin's eyes moved slowly over her. He wasn't, she realised as she stood still under his scrutiny, trying not to show her resentment of it, the man she'd wondered if he might be — the man who didn't even notice she was a woman. He was noticing that all right — noticing it rather too appreciatively, and she tried to combat his assessment with one of her own, letting her own green eyes rove over his face, taking in the saturnine good looks, the brows that could have been forbidding if it hadn't been for that slight quirk at their outer ends, the straight nose, the eyes that glittered like splinters of broken ice; the thin, chiselled lips that were now set uncompromisingly firm but looked as if they could express a compelling sensuality . . . Rachel brought herself up short. What on earth was she thinking? She caught Lorne Quentin's glance on her cheeks and felt their warmth. Curse the man — he had her at a disadvantage already, without even trying!

But when he spoke, Lorne Quentin's voice didn't reveal any awareness of an advantage. Nor did it express any prejudice. It was as deep as she had subconsciously expected it to be, but it was mild, even friendly, with a pleasant warmth that caught her completely off guard.

"Please sit down," he said, and when she had done so: "You're Rachel Grant? Married?"

"Single." He must have that on her file already, she'd filled in a comprehensive application form as well as completing her own curriculum vitae. But she recognised that he was merely talking to put her at ease, warming her up before the real interview began. She wondered if he would have the impertinence to enquire any fur-

14

ther into her private life, as some employers did. At some of her previous interviews, Rachel had been asked whether she intended marriage, whether she was living with anyone, even whether she planned to have a family. She braced herself to give Lorne Quentin short shrift if he dared to do the same.

However, he did nothing of the kind, although there was definitely something — curiosity, perhaps — in those cool eyes. Was he wondering just how an attractive woman got to nearly twenty-eight and escaped marriage? Well, she could tell him that but it would take too long and anyway Rachel wasn't a girl to bare her soul to every stranger who wondered about her. Or to anyone at all now, she thought, and stifled a sigh.

"And you've applied for the position of Assistant Designer with my company," he went on, still in the cool, flat voice that nevertheless seemed to hint at some hidden warmth. "What made you do that, Miss Grant?"

"I wanted the job." She just prevented her tone from showing that she thought this a silly question, but saw from the quirk of one dark brow that he hadn't missed the implication.

"I rather gathered that. Yet you already hold a very responsible position with Britton Cars. Why do you want to leave them?"

Rachel shrugged. "In many ways, I don't. I've enjoyed working there and I believe I've done some good work. But I want to do something," she hesitated, "more individual. More exciting. Britton Cars are very much for the family motorist, and I'd like to branch out, do something different."

"And you think Quentin Motors are likely to help you do that? We seem to do very well with our basic design, which many people might consider old-fashioned. As indeed it is — we haven't changed it much for the past twenty-five years."

"I know." Rachel thought of the classic Quentin — it had never even needed another name — a low-slung sports car with long bonnet and a racy shape that was entirely its own, recognisable anywhere, timeless rather than old-fashioned, its throaty roar and powerful acceleration as characteristic as its shape. "But I'd heard you were considering some new lines — cars that would be just as much Quentin, yet entirely different. It sounds exciting and I'd like to be in on it."

"You would, would you?" Lorne Quentin considered her, his eyes gleaming almost silver under the thick brows. Rachel looked back steadily. He wasn't conventionally handsome, she thought irrelevantly, the craggy sternness of his face saw to that. But those eyes, that firm mouth, the unexpected silkiness of the black hair that contoured the fine shape of his head, all of these added up to something unforgettable. And implacable. She shivered suddenly, aware of a tiny note of warning somewhere in her mind.

"So, Quentin Motors are what you've been looking for," he mused, his deep voice almost gentle. "But are *you* what Quentin Motors have been looking for, Miss Grant? That's what you have to persuade us of." And he smiled.

He doesn't think I can, Rachel thought suddenly. He's invited me to come for interview out of little more than curiosity — to see what a woman car designer looks like. And just in case I *might* be good enough to interest him — after all, he knows my qualifications and experience, and they must count for *something*. But he doesn't really believe I can be innovative enough for Quentin's new lines, or brilliant enough to match up to his own standards.

In fact, he's already made up his mind about me.

She felt her temper rise. All right, so Lorne Quentin hadn't exhibited any of the usual prejudice or hostility, the kind of attitudes she'd come to expect and learned to cope with. But bringing her here for little more than amusement, that was just as bad, in her book. And she determined that before she left here this afternoon, either with or without the job, she would make the owner of Quentin Motors laugh on the other side of his face. In the nicest possible way, of course, she acknowledged with a hidden smile. There wasn't going to be any slanging match and he would never know just how angry she might be inside. Rachel had a temper that went with the fiery colour of her hair, but it wasn't often nowadays that anyone saw it in action. That was something she'd learned to control on her way up.

"Well," she said, keeping her voice light and pleasant, "tell me just what you want to know. All you have to do is ask, after all. The decision then is yours."

She saw Lorne's glance flick towards Mike Dalton, and felt a tiny shock of surprise. The power of his personality had been such that she had completely forgotten there was anyone else in the room with them. She turned her head, and saw the Chief Designer watching her. His face was as impassive as Lorne Quentin's — or nearly so. Wasn't that a tiny glimmer of approval she saw in the blue eyes?

Encouraged, she turned back to Lorne and gave him her most charming smile — not that she wanted to *charm* him, she told herself quickly — the smile was simply an overture of friendliness, designed to make him respond to her. Along with a good many other business men and women, Rachel had attended more than one course in management — 'how to win friends and influence people' — and knew the value of the soft sell. Whether you were selling yourself — your skills, ability, knowledge — or a product, it invariably worked better than the aggressive stance that was now out of date.

"What would you like to know?" she enquired softly, and caught the brief flicker in Lorne's eyes, though she still wasn't sure what it meant. Approval, or more amusement? Outwardly pliant, inside she became steel.

"Perhaps you'd like to tell us about your experience," Mike Dalton suggested, his voice warm. "I know we've got it all on

19

paper, but you can expand on the brief notes here. You started off at college, didn't you?"

"Yes — a polytechnic." Rachel launched into a potted biography of herself, talking about her training in both engineering and design, her interest in cars and her desire to evolve something that was both advanced and functional, practical yet stylish. As she talked, her face lit up with an enthusiasm that had been impossible to commit to paper, and she went on to explain how she'd worked her way up the ladder until obtaining her present position with Britton Cars. Quite an achievement, she'd believed, and it was evident that Mike thought so too — but when she glanced again at Lorne Quentin, he was looking distinctly unimpressed.

"And now you're prepared to give Quentin Motors the benefit of your expertise?" he enquired, and Rachel flushed at the faintly sardonic note of his voice. She wondered if she had allowed her enthusiasm to run away with her and had ended up sounding conceited and brash. But Mike's interested blue eyes and responsive nods had been so encouraging, she'd almost forgotten she was having an interview.

"I don't think I ever said that, Mr Quentin," she returned coolly. "I hope to be useful, of course. I hope I can bring quite a lot to the firm if you decide to appoint me. But I'd look forward to learning a lot too. I've already told you, I want to get on — I'm ambitious."

"Ambitious?" he drawled, and this time the amusement in his eyes was unmistakable as he glanced again at his Chief Designer. "You'd better watch out, Mike — you could be fighting off a determined contender for your own job." His glance returned to Rachel. "But isn't ambition rather an *unfeminine* attribute?"

"Unfeminine?" she retorted. "I don't see why. I'm sure I don't have to remind you that we're in the nineteen-nineties, Mr Quentin. Women can take up most careers now, *and* succeed at them. And it doesn't mean they have to lose their femininity."

"No, I'm sure you're right," he murmured, and his eyes moved over her slender, curving body again, lifting to study her pale, ivory face and sparkling eyes. "So long as they don't *use* their femininity in a way that's unfair to the men they work with."

"You mean in the way that so many men unfairly use their masculinity?" Rachel

21

enquired sweetly. "Sexual harassment, I believe it's called, — rife in offices especially — though now that a few women have dared to bring it to the public notice, it might just die down a little." She gave Lorne Quentin a glance that was as cool as his own, green ice meeting silver. "No, Mr Quentin, I don't use my femininity as a weapon at work. I don't think about differences of sex in the drawing-office. But neither do I see any need to deny that I *am* a woman, by dressing like a pseudo-man, in masculine suits or trousers. That, to my mind, shows a preoccupation with gender just as much as if I were to wear low-cut blouses and split skirts."

Lorne stared at her for a moment, then to her astonishment flung back his head and gave a burst of laughter. Rachel looked back at him, nonplussed, not sure whether to be angry or join in his amusement. She glanced at Mike and saw that his lips too were twitching, and she allowed herself a smile, acknowledging that while she had been expressing exactly what she believed, she might, perhaps, have sounded just a touch pompous. At the same time she realised that she was actually enjoying this sparring with Lorne Quentin, and she had a strong feeling that he was enjoying it too.

"All right," she said in a more relaxed voice when Lorne's laughter had died down. "So it sounds funny, put like that. But doesn't it make sense?"

"It surely does," he agreed, his voice betraying the fact that he might start to chuckle all over again. "I'm sorry, Miss Grant. It was just the idea of you in a pin-stripe suit, with a bowler hat . . ." His voice shook and she restrained the impulse to tell him that such outfits had only recently been high fashion. "No, I'm sure you're right. And if you'll forgive me being personal, your dress today indicates that you have very feminine tastes indeed. Now, how the hell did we get into this conversation?" He frowned. "Oh, of course — ambition." He became businesslike again, but there was a distinct lessening of tension in the air and Rachel began to wonder if she might dare to hope that there was a chance for her. "I'd just like to know a little more about your ideas regarding current designs." He began to question her closely; so closely that the tiny flicker of hope faltered, and then died altogether. Rachel didn't dare to glance at her watch as she fumbled for answers, but she was aware that she must have been in here already for a good deal longer than the previous applicant. Whether that was a good sign or not, she didn't know, but she didn't think it was. No, Lorne Quentin was bending over backwards to give her no reason to complain about prejudice. He was giving her an interview so thorough that she would never be able to say he'd dismissed her application out of hand. And at the same time, amongst all the discussion and argument they were now embarking on, he was sure to be able to find some good reason why he couldn't offer her the position.

When you looked at it like that, the whole thing was as much a farce as if he had simply told her outright that he didn't intend to appoint her, but had simply invited her for interview just for form's sake. Except that if he'd done that, she could at least have had the satisfaction of losing her temper. This way, he was being so reasonable that she couldn't — much as she would have liked to.

"Well, I think that just about covers everything," he said at last, leaning back in his chair. "Anything further you'd like to ask, Mike? No? Miss Grant, anything you'd like to know that we've left out?"

"No, I think you've been very thorough." Just let me get out of here, she thought grimly, wondering if there were any part of her background that Lorne Quentin hadn't explored. But that was silly, of course there was. One quite significant part, which she'd never mentioned and didn't intend to. That part of her life was none of Lorne's business, whatever he might suppose.

"Then I think we'll call it a day for now." His eyes were a warmer grey now, the shade of dove's wings, as he smiled at her. Switching on his social personality, she thought cynically, aware of her own involuntary response to a smile that lit up the dark face, making it seem suddenly ten years younger. "Mike will show you round the factory and the offices. But first, you must be dying for a cup of tea." He pressed the intercom on his desk and turned the smile to the secretary who came in from the outer office. "Tea, please, Julie. And some chocolate biscuits — we've earned them."

Rachel waited warily. Did tea and chocolate biscuits mean she'd got the job, or were they a kind of consolation prize? Or was it just tea-time anyway? She responded politely to Lorne Quentin's small-talk, telling him that no, she'd never been to this part of Herefordshire before, she tended to spend weekends in the Cotswolds or back home in Devon with her family, and yes, she had been abroad on holiday this year, to Switzerland. Not for the skiing, no, but she hoped to go next winter with a friend who was keen . . . She was relieved when Julie arrived with the tea, served in bone-china cups, and although she seldom ate biscuits, she was grateful for the comfort of a chocolate one today. As soon as she had drunk one cup and could leave politely, she'd do so. By now, she was convinced that Lorne Quentin had no intention of making her his Assistant Designer. And it wasn't just his attitude during the interview, that had been impeccable. No, there was something else — some undercurrent that she didn't understand. Something that made the air crackle between them, something that made her just a little too aware of the force of his personality. Something that told her that while he would certainly be stimulating to work with, the stimulation would be of such an intensity that it had to be dangerous — like getting hold of a high-voltage cable.

She followed Mike out of the office, leaving Lorne's cool inscrutability behind for what she felt was a less rarefied atmosphere. But although his personality

26

seemed to be everywhere, an all-pervasive dominance, she became conscious as they toured the factory of a deep longing to be part of it all — part of the close-knit atmosphere that bonded the employees, whether in the offices or on the factory floor, into something very like a family. From all of them — from the youngest apprentice to the oldest foreman — emanated the same solid pride in the job and in Quentin's itself.

"It's because Quentin's has been here so long," Mike explained when she commented on this. "An old family firm, into three generations, in what would otherwise be an area of low employment — it's part of the scenery. And the old tradition of looking after the estate and its workers has been carried over into the factory. Here's someone who can tell you that better than I can — Arthur Morris. He's been here all his life — due to retire this summer." Mike indicated the leather-faced little man who was carefully polishing a completed car, making it ready to go out to an owner who had probably been waiting patiently for two years. "Arthur always likes to see that the cars are perfect when they leave here, don't you, Arthur?"

"That's right." The bent back straightened and the creased face reflected back from the car's long, shining bonnet. "Done this job since I were a nipper. Mind, it isn't my real work now, but I likes to do it. It's like a sort of bonus for me, you might say."

"What is your real work, then?" Rachel asked, and listened with interest as Arthur explained in meticulous detail. He was clearly a craftsman, taking pride in every aspect of his work, with no time at all for shirkers.

"Doesn't matter if no one ever sees it," he declared, and Rachel knew that this must be one of his favourite sayings, "you knows yourself if it be done proper or not, and if it isn't," he shrugged, "well, that's a day of your life wasted, that's what I say."

It was an attitude far different from that of the production line at Britton's, or almost any other large car factory she had known. But here it seemed to be common-place. There was a caring, almost a loving, in the way the cars were built, a loving that would carry over into their lives on the road. Quentin cars were invariably well looked-after, their owners as enthusiastic about them as the owners of veterans. And many of them were veterans, of course, for Quentin's had been built to last. Planned obsolescence didn't come into Quentin designs, and never had.

"It's an incredible place," she said, half to herself; then, turning back to Arthur: "And you've worked here all your life?"

"That's right. Come here as a boy, I did, when old Mr Quentin started up. That were Mr Lorne's grandad, of course. He were gettin' on a bit by then and Mr Andrew worked with him, they built it up together like. But I be the only man left that started with them."

"And you're retiring soon? I hope they give you a good send-off," Rachel said with a smile.

"Oh, we shall," Mike said as they moved away. "Lorne believes in looking after his employees, and Arthur's rather special. It's a good place to work, you know. Happy atmosphere. I suppose it's because we're relatively small and we produce a low number of cars. People have got time to take pride in what they do. At the big factories, no one ever sees more than a tiny part of each car. Here we take an interest in the whole vehicle."

"Arthur's a real craftsman, anyone can see that," Rachel said thoughtfully. "He loves what he's doing. It probably breaks his heart to see a car leave!"

Mike laughed. "You could be right — especially if the customer doesn't match up to his idea of what a Quentin owner should be. Well — seen enough?"

"Oh yes." Enough, Rachel thought wistfully, to know that Quentin Motors was the one place she wanted to work. But she didn't entertain any hope that she would get the job. Lorne Quentin's face, when she returned to his office to say goodbye, was as inscrutable as ever, and his eyes were veiled as he rose to shake her hand.

He had satisfied his curiosity about her; he had enjoyed sparring with her during the interview; he might even be quite impressed by her qualifications. But appoint her? That seemed very unlikely. And there wasn't a thing Rachel could do about it, other than remain as cool and poised as he. There was no need for him to *know* just how badly she wanted to work for him.

As she drove away, she felt like a child at Christmas, seeing the most coveted present on the tree going to someone else; knowing that they wouldn't delight in it half as much as she would have done; knowing that it ought to have been hers.

It was just a job, she told herself, resolutely turning her thoughts away. There would be others. It was a job, that was all.

All the same, she couldn't quite dismiss from her thoughts the image of a dark, craggy face that could be lit with a smile that was like the sun coming out. Of cool, silvery eyes that could suddenly sparkle with humour. And of something else — something she couldn't quite recognise, yet felt she ought to.

Not that it was any good wondering about it. She would probably never meet Lorne Quentin again.

Two

The knock came just as Rachel was putting the final touches to some drawings, brought home to finish in the peace and quiet that so rarely existed in her bustling office at Britton's. She gave a last glance at her papers, then went to open the door, wondering who was there. Probably one of the girls from upstairs with an invitation to coffee, she thought, or maybe that new young man who'd moved in below her to borrow something or ask where the nearest delicatessen was. That was typical of living in a flat and whether you liked it or not depended on your own nature. Some people might love the cosy 'family' atmosphere, others would find it unbearably claustrophobic.

But it wasn't the new young man who stood at her door; neither was it one of the girls from upstairs. For a moment, when she saw who it was, Rachel felt as if everything had stopped. Her heartbeat, her breath, life itself. Only her eyes continued to function — and what they were telling her just couldn't be true.

Lorne Quentin's head reached a good three inches higher than any of her previous visitors'. His broad shoulders seemed almost to fill the space of the doorway; his lean body, tapering to narrow hips and long legs, looked as dangerous and potent as the blade of a rapier, scabbarded in the dark business suit he wore. The colour accentuated the raven blackness of his hair and brows, and against them his eyes glittered more silvery than ever.

"Can I come in?" he asked when Rachel had gazed at him for several speechless moments.

"Er . . . yes, yes, of course." She cursed her voice, which was as shaky and tremulous as some moonstruck teenager's. "I'm sorry, you took me by surprise. I didn't expect to see you here . . . or . . ."

"Or ever again?" he finished for her. "No, I don't suppose you did. I rather got that impression when you left my office last week. You'd quite made up your mind I wasn't going to appoint you, hadn't you?"

"Well?" Rachel had recovered herself quickly — at least enough to be able to speak without stuttering. She tilted her head back and sent him a challenging glance. "And wasn't I right?"

"Let's waive that question for the

moment, shall we?" Lorne closed the door behind him and stepped through her tiny hall and into the main room of the flat. "Hm. Nice place you have here. It's your own, is it?"

"Mine and the building society's." Rachel followed his glance around the room. "Yes, it's rather nice, isn't it? I like these older blocks, and this one has been very well-modernised. I believe it was originally a hotel, but you wouldn't know it now. And every flat is different."

Lorne nodded, his eyes taking in the gracefully moulded cornices and attractive fireplace. The room was pleasantly proportioned, with a high ceiling and large bay window in which Rachel had collected a display of potted plants. The floor was close-carpeted in tones of rich burgundy, picked up in the long velvet curtains, which gave warmth to the plain white walls. Full bookshelves and a few good pictures denoted her tastes, and an expensive music centre stood in one corner, with a few CDs scattered around it that showed it was not just an ornament. Two squashy sofas faced each other by the fireplace, one strewn with books and papers, while at the other side of the room stood the drawing-board Rachel kept permanently in position for the work she brought home.

She stood waiting for Lorne Quentin to finish his survey, grateful for the breathing space. It had been a considerable shock to see him at her door, but she wasn't sure just what kind of shock. There seemed to be a mixture of emotions churning about inside her, and she needed time to sort them out.

For instance, could it really have been a blaze of joy that she had felt at her first incredulous recognition? All right, so she hadn't actually *disliked* Lorne at that interview — he'd impressed her as both an employer and a man — but that didn't mean she had to react quite so violently, did it?

It was difficult to tell. That first flare of emotion had been so quickly followed by disbelief, by a caution as positive as the drawing in of a snail's horns, by a clang of warning in her mind that this man could spell danger. And this by a rapid, scornful rebuttal. What possible danger could Lorne Quentin present to her? But that, she thought warily, could depend on why he had come.

Rachel sighed and moved away. Since the interview last week she'd worked quite hard to put Lorne Quentin — and his job, she added hastily — right out of her mind. She wasn't going to be his Assistant Designer, she believed that had been made perfectly clear by the cool, polite way he had terminated the interview and by the fact that she'd heard nothing since. That being the case, there was no reason why she should ever come in contact with Lorne again; he would once again become an almost legendary figure in her world, heard about only in terms of success, with the occasional mention in the gossip columns as he escorted some beauty to a nightclub or party. And that didn't happen all that often; Lorne Quentin wasn't known for being a socialite, which was what made him all the more interesting and enigmatic to the writers of such columns.

A sudden wry smile twisted her lips as Rachel wondered if that was why he was here — to ask her for a date. That would set the tongues wagging — the owner of Quentin Motors escorting one of the senior designers of Britton Cars! She could just see the reaction of her present boss, on opening his newspaper one morning to see those headlines and the accompanying picture. He'd have her in his office before you could say carburettor, to find out just what design secrets she'd been passing — or acquiring. Well, there wasn't any danger of *that* happening. Only Rachel herself knew just how well she was armed against industrial espionage.

She turned her head to find Lorne watching her, his brows drawn together quizzically. The cool grey eyes gleamed.

"So, what were you going to do if you did come to work for us?" he asked, and she realised that he was still referring to the flat. "Sell it?"

Rachel shrugged. "Probably, once I was sure the job would work out. A friend was anxious to rent it for a few months while she looked around for her own place. I wasn't looking ahead too far at that point."

His brows rose, turning up at the outer corners in a way that gave him an unexpected leprechaun look. "Weren't you? I got the impression that you were a lady who had everything buttoned up." His eyes dropped to her shirt, its top three buttons unfastened to reveal a shadowy cleft. "Well, almost everything!" he added with a hint of laughter in his voice, his smile inviting her to laugh with him.

Rachel struggled briefly with herself and then turned away. Let this man get under her guard, and the hidden undercurrent of danger she had sensed could become more than a hint. She moved towards the kitchen door, hearing her voice sounding marvellously cool as she offered him coffee. "Do have a good look around," she added graciously, with a glance over her shoulder, letting him see that she found his survey of the room a little too interested to be altogether polite. "I'll show you the rest of the flat later, if you like."

His brows were up again, but he said nothing, only accepted her offer of coffee in a voice whose politeness matched her own. We're going to play it my way, she thought triumphantly, and then wondered what the game was anyway. Or was it a game? It was beginning to feel perilously like a battle — a battle over some issue she didn't even understand.

In the kitchen, Rachel closed the door and leaned against it, brushing a few tendrils of flame-coloured hair back from her forehead. Why had he come? And why did she have to be looking like this when he did come — hair loose and unruly, old shirt and jeans, no make-up? She remembered his teasing look and hastily fastened two buttons. The shirt was one that had shrunk at sometime in the wash and strained across her breasts in a way that

38

was hardly modest. She sighed and undid one of the buttons again, jumping guiltily as Lorne opened the door behind her.

"Sorry, I was just wondering if I could help." Rachel felt her cheeks flame as she saw his eyes go to the newly-fastened button, and bit her own lip as she saw his mouth twitch. But before she could speak, he had removed his gaze and was blandly inspecting the kitchen. "Yes, a very convenient layout. Did you design it yourself?" He moved across to the window. "Pity about the view, though — or do you prefer to be surrounded by other buildings? If so, I'm afraid you'd have found the quiet of our part of Herefordshire a little eerie. People do, I'm told, when they come from the city. Owls and things, you know." He turned and gave her the smile that so disturbingly lit up his austere face.

Rachel filled the coffee-jug and switched on. "I'm accustomed to living in the country, Mr Quentin," she told him. "I grew up in a village on Exmoor. I don't think the Herefordshire countryside would have frightened me." Sadly, she realised that they were both using *would have* in referring to the job. So he hadn't come to offer it to her. Not that she'd really allowed herself to hope, but still . . .

39

"Exmoor?" He looked at her with real interest now. "I've spent quite a lot of time around that way myself. Used to have relatives in Minehead. Your family live there?"

"Yes." Rachel turned to get out mugs, milk and sugar. She set them on a tray, thankful to have something to do. Lorne's presence in her tiny kitchen was distinctly overwhelming. "My father's a doctor. I grew up on the moor with my brothers. We spent all our holidays roaming about — it was our playground."

"Lucky you," he remarked. "A real family childhood." Rachel gave him a quick glance — had there been a touch of wistfulness in his tone? "And are your brothers engineers, too?"

"No. Tim's a lawyer, Andrew's an accountant and Jonathan's a doctor, like Dad." Rachel took mugs from a cupboard and set them on a tray. "Sugar, Mr Quentin? And a chocolate biscuit?" She produced the tin kept for visitors, thinking that it was ironic that she should be offering him the same little delicacy he had given her. Catching his glance, she realised that he had noticed it too. Her hand shook a little as she lifted the tray. Was he a mind-reader, or had they just happened to think along the same wavelength?

40

Danger, the bell clanged again in her mind. This man is danger.

"Don't you think you could drop the 'Mr Quentin' bit now?" Lorne asked, following her back into the room. He moved with an indolent, feline ease, the well-cut dark suit immaculately tailored for his lean, muscular body. "I'd like to call you Rachel, if you've no objection."

Rachel shrugged, implying that it couldn't matter less what he called her. "Everyone uses first names now, don't you find?" she said lightly. "Perhaps you'd like to sit there. Do you like it black or white?"

"A touch of milk." He watched as she poured, then reached out a tapering hand to take the mug from her. Their fingers barely touched and Rachel let go of the mug so rapidly that she was afraid he would drop it. Her heart kicked as she sat down and reached for her own drink. In God's name, what on earth was the matter with her? She was a mature woman, not a smitten teenager. And she *wasn't* smitten. All right, Lorne Quentin had more than his fair share of sex appeal, but that was all. *All.* Acknowledge it, and then ignore it. There was no reason on earth why she should let it get to her. He wasn't the first man she'd found attractive, not by a long chalk.

Lorne certainly didn't seem to be affected in the same way by her. He leaned back in his seat, crossing his legs and sipping his coffee. Rachel sat opposite him, outwardly calm, wondering again why he had come. Was he ever going to tell her?

"Have — have you been in Birmingham on business?" she asked at last, keeping her tone casual, and he flicked her a bright, silvery glance.

"Yes. And since I was in the area, I thought I'd call in and see you." He sipped again and Rachel tightened her fingers around her cup in exasperation. "This is very good coffee, Rachel."

"I'm glad you like it." She let her eyes drift over to the drawing-board standing at the side of the room. "I was just going to have a break anyway." If he wasn't going to tell her why he'd come — it surely wasn't just for coffee! — she was going to make it plain he was interrupting her evening.

Lorne followed her glance. "Oh, you were working. I won't ask if I can see." His eyes glittered wickedly. "I'm sure it's some revolutionary new design that you're keeping a deadly secret from rivals."

"Do you know," Rachel said after a tiny pause, "I find that just a shade patronising."

Lorne gave her a quick glance, then his mobile mouth curled in a grin. "So it was," he admitted cheerfully. "I can see you're not a lady to allow liberties."

Rachel shrugged, feeling more in control now. She remembered the reluctant pleasure she'd got from their sparring at the interview. If she could only keep things on that level. There was, after all, no reason at all why she should let this man upset her, no reason either why she should pull her punches. She wasn't going to work for him, after all; nor was she about to start an affair with him, if that was what he had in mind. "I don't bother much about liberties," she remarked. "In my working life I just expect to be treated as a colleague. It's as simple as that."

"Really?" he murmured. "And in your private life?"

Rachel looked down at her slim fingers. They were ringless, still pale from the winter, the nails short but coloured with a soft pink. She found herself glancing involuntarily at Lorne's hands, comparing the long, capable fingers, the powerful wrists . . . "My private life is my own business," she said a little jerkily.

Lorne inclined his head. "Agreed. But you do *have* a private life, I take it? I was just wondering — if you were to come to Herefordshire, isn't there anyone here who'd miss you? Or is that a patronising question too?"

"Insulting, I would have said, though I'm sure you didn't mean it to be." Rachel gave him a steady look. "I have friends, yes." But she knew he hadn't meant that. He'd been asking if there were anyone special — and there could be only one reason for that. All her instincts were crowding in on her now, telling her not to get involved with this man, not to let him get close. Danger, they intoned, *danger* . . .

As she met Lorne's eyes, she felt a tiny shock at the expression she saw there. It wasn't one she could immediately recognise. Interest — but what kind of interest? Not simply the interest of a virile man for an attractive woman. There was that, yes, but there was something else too. Something she'd seen before and now couldn't name.

It had been in the eyes of a friend, long ago. After . . . She tore her mind away.

"I don't have a lover, if that's what you're asking," she said quietly. "Nor any plans to include one in my life." She paused to let that sink in, then stood up, trembling a little. This conversation was proving a considerable strain and she wanted to end it. Her eyes fell on her drawing-board, and she felt an odd rush of relief in having some legitimate cause for anger, for venting some of her confused feelings. "And now, if you don't mind, I'd like to get back to my work. You haven't given me any reason for coming here other than that you were in the area and fancied a cup of coffee. Maybe you wanted to see what that curious breed, a woman car designer, looked like at home — perhaps you thought I was some kind of robot, switched off for the night and ready to start again next morning when someone plugs me in." She spoke quickly, deliberately whipping up her indignation to begin with, until it took over and became real anger. "Well, as you can see, I'm quite ordinary, just like anyone else. So if you've finished your coffee and there's nothing else you want — a sandwich, perhaps? Or maybe a four-course meal? — perhaps you'd go and leave me to get on with my work. Because I've got quite a lot to do, and all of it more interesting than what I'm doing at the moment!"

She braked to a halt, glowering at him, unaware of the effect of her snapping green eyes and flame of hair that tumbled around

45

her oval face. Her breasts thrust against the shirt that was still too tightly buttoned over them, and she was suddenly conscious of Lorne's eyes on them as they rose and fell with her quickened breathing. Dimly, she was also aware that she had spoken much more rudely than she'd intended — something that always happened when she lost her temper, rare though that was nowadays. Feeling at a distinct disadvantage, and flushing with annoyance, she fumed away, feeling a sting of frustrated tears in her eyes.

"All right, Rachel." Lorne's voice was unexpectedly gentle, catching her off-guard yet again. "Sit down. You've made your point. I'm sorry I annoyed you."

Rachel turned back and looked down at him uncertainly. He held out his hand, indicating that she should return to the sofa, and she sat down slowly opposite him.

"I imagine you must have had your fair share of teasing, with three brothers," he remarked, setting down his cup. "Tell me a bit more about yourself, Rachel. How did you come to end up in engineering? Didn't you ever think of medicine yourself?"

Still doubtful, Rachel took a mouthful of coffee, swallowed it and decided to answer him. Presumably this was all leading up to *something*, and she owed Lorne a little courtesy, at least, for his calm reaction to her outburst. "I went through the usual stage of wanting to be a nurse. But it didn't last any longer with me than with most small girls. Ponies became more important. But, well, I always did have a passion for engines. Anything mechanical. I was always the one who wanted to take things apart to see how they worked. I used to swop my dolls for my brother Jonathan's Meccano sets. My Sindy doll and cuddly animals ended up having operations, while I built cranes and water-wheels and model aircraft."

"But there must have been more to it than that. Children play at all sorts of things — they don't necessarily end up making a career of them. For instance, you must have had encouragement. And you must have had discouragement as well, just because you were a girl."

"Yes, I did. Not so much discouragement — though my mother was very much aware of the difficulties of a girl going into engineering. But then, she would have because she'd spent her own working years in a mostly male environment as an assistant in a forensic laboratory, and knew that a woman had to be twice as good as any man if she were to get on. She believed in me, though. She never let me think that the way would be easy, but she gave me the courage to try."

"And your father? Your brothers?" Lorne was leaning forward in his seat now, his grey eyes bright. Rachel gave him a wary glance. Could he *really* be interested in all this?

"Dad's always taken the attitude that anyone who really wants to do something probably can. Children who long to write, paint, make music — he says they're almost invariably equipped, mentally and physically, to do just those things. Pianists with long fingers," she couldn't help an involuntary glance at Lorne's own long, sensitive hands, "runners with long legs, actors with rubber faces who can make themselves look like anyone they choose —" she broke off, aware that enthusiasm was once again taking her over. It was all part of the effect Lorne had on her, she thought, and determined to temper her responses. She'd learned over the years to play it cool, keep her feelings and reactions very much to herself. So why did he have the power to break down her barriers, without even trying?

"So you were encouraged to go in for engineering," he mused, and Rachel nodded.

"Most of all by an uncle, who was a civil engineer himself. He knew the difficulties too, but I suppose he could also see some potential in me. I didn't actually have to fight my way in," she admitted with a smile, "at least, not until I got to poly and found myself the only girl on the course."

"And when you had to start fighting for jobs," he supplied, and Rachel nodded again. She watched as Lorne drained the last of his coffee. Could they now be getting to the point of his visit?

"I felt somewhat guilty about you the other day," he said then, startlingly. "That interview — I really put you under the grill. I realised afterwards that I hadn't treated any of the male applicants like that. I'm never soft at interviews, anyone who comes to work for me has to prove himself — or herself! But with you, yes, I was tougher. Though I didn't actually see it until afterwards, when Mike pointed it out to me."

"There wasn't any need to come and apologise," Rachel heard herself saying stiffly. "As you've guessed, I'm quite accustomed to prejudice in all its forms.

49

Unless you really came to confirm that, so that you could tell yourself you're no worse than the next man."

Lorne laughed, his white teeth flashing in the darkness of his face. "Oh lord, here we go again. Misunderstandings — how I hate them. And how easily — and usually unnecessarily — they arise. All right, Rachel, I'll come clean with you. No, I didn't come to apologise. Nor did I come to tease you, admire your flat, drink your coffee or waste your time." His eyes were deeper now, almost sombre, and his face was serious as he looked at her over the low coffee-table. "I came to offer you the job of Assistant Designer at Quentin Motors. As a matter of fact, there's a letter in the post on its way to you now — you'll probably receive it in the morning. But as I said, I was in Birmingham and I suddenly felt I'd like to offer it to you face-to-face. I hope you're still interested in accepting it."

Rachel stared at him. The breath seemed to have been punched from her body. Lorne's face blurred, then came clear again and became the only steady point in a whirling room. There was a roaring in her ears, a rhythmic surging. Slowly, it faded; the room steadied. Lorne was still watching her, a faint smile on his face, his brows quirking.

"Perhaps you need time to think it over," he said. "It's a big step. Leaving Britton's — it's a good job you've got there. Leaving this pleasant flat. I don't really expect you to decide immediately."

Rachel found her voice.

"But I've decided. I decided when I applied for the post. I told you I wanted it."

"And nothing's happened to change your mind? The interview? Seeing the factory, the office you'd be working in, the area where you'd live?" His pause was infinitesimal. "Seeing me?"

Rachel looked at him. She thought of the factory, set in the grounds of Lorne Quentin's own family home, so cleverly landscaped that it was invisible to the surrounding countryside. She thought of the offices, a part of the house itself, yet still spacious and modern. She thought of the Herefordshire villages she had passed through, their tranquillity, the black and white timbered cottages that had stood there for centuries.

She looked at Lorne, and once again heard that warning bell in her mind. Could she really work with him? Wasn't she being

51

just a bit crazy even to think of trying?

Because Lorne Quentin had, she knew, an overpowering attraction for her. An attraction so strong that he couldn't fail to be aware of it himself. And that, in a working environment, could only spell danger.

Danger was something Rachel had never been afraid of. A few years ago, in her eager teens and early twenties the heady excitement of her feelings about Lorne would have been something she'd have explored with all the recklessness that went with her tempestuous nature. The possible consequences would have played no part in her calculations.

But all that was over. Rachel no longer played life by ear. Experience, she'd discovered, was a hard school. It had taught her quite a lot, especially about men like Lorne.

Working with him could be more than dangerous. It could prove a disaster.

Three

Lorne wasn't in the staff dining-room when Rachel went in for lunch, and she heaved a small sigh of relief. She was well aware that the appointment of a woman to her post had caused some speculation, speculation which appeared frequently in the eyes of her colleagues. She was still new enough at Quentin Motors, too, to be interesting in herself — and Lorne, of course, was always interesting.

A wry smile tugged her lips at the thought. To say that Lorne Quentin was merely "interesting" must be the understatement of all time. Practically every woman in the factory was at least a quarter in love with him, if only as a fantasy figure. And that wasn't really surprising when you took into account his craggily handsome face, the dark hair that shaped his head, the way those piercing grey eyes could soften into warmth when his stern lips occasionally relaxed and curled into a leprechaun devilment that twisted the heart. Not many women were immune to that kind of charm.

Not even Rachel Grant, she acknowledged as she sat down at a small table and studied the day's menu. And through her relief, she was conscious of a stab of regret that he wasn't here to share her meal.

The staff dining-room was a small annexe off the main canteen, a quiet oasis from the hubbub, served by two waitresses. One of them came across to Rachel now and took her order. Rachel gave it in an abstracted tone, barely aware of what she was choosing. Once again, Lorne Quentin had invaded her thoughts and this time she was disposed to let him. Pushing him out every time his face had risen to haunt her mind hadn't worked, after all. So why not accept the inevitable, let her mind have full rein and see if that got him out of her system?

Even now, after almost a month at Quentin Motors, Rachel was still confused about the exact nature of her relationship with her employer. She was, if anything, even more confused than she had been during that last month at Britton Cars, while she was working out her notice. Then, she had confidently expected that when she started at Quentin's everything would sort itself out and that she and

Lorne would quickly develop a satisfactory working relationship, become colleagues with the same easy comradeship that she was accustomed to. But it hadn't worked out that way.

Maybe it was all the fault of that little warning bell in her mind, the one that had kept clanging 'danger'. Rachel shrugged impatiently, as if some irritating insect kept settling on her. She'd been too strung-up that night, tense after a week's waiting to hear about the job, making up her mind she hadn't got it, so that Lorne's arrival at her door had thrown her completely — particularly when he had taken so long to get around to telling her he was appointing her, teasing her along, enjoying her suspense. She still hadn't completely forgiven him for that.

As for that danger — well, he was an attractive man. He wasn't the only one in the world, there were plenty of others and Rachel had met her share. She wasn't usually so strongly affected, it was true, she'd had enough experience to overcome that, but it was surely only a matter of degree. Physical attraction, that was all it was. It meant nothing, and after a while it passed.

He wasn't even the only one in the factory. Mike Dalton, for instance, with his fair hair, friendly blue eyes and pleasant smile, he was every bit as good-looking as Lorne, maybe even more so. And that was the difference, she thought, smiling absently at the waitress who brought her salad. Mike was good-looking, friendly, nice. But what Lorne had wasn't really to do with good looks and it was nothing at all to do with being nice. It was a dark, devastating attraction that spelled excitement, adventure and danger. Mike, she decided, was the kind of man girls married. Lorne was most definitely not. He was the kind women had affairs with.

And that was why her instincts had cried 'danger'. Because Rachel was all too well aware of her own responses. For her, an affair could never be enough. All right, there could be joy, ecstasy, rapture, but there must also, inevitably, be pain and despair. She didn't want it, she didn't want anything to do with it.

And there was Lorne's own nature — the dark, powerful side of him that she knew only from intuition, the side that called out to a part of her that she kept hidden even from herself. From the first, she had known that if Lorne and she were to embark on an affair it would make Antony and Cleopatra look like Darby and Joan.

The joy might be more intense, but so would be the pain.

No, the risks were too great. Affairs — and particularly affairs with men like Lorne Quentin — were out.

It hadn't always been like that, she thought wryly, but at least she'd learned from her past mistakes. They'd been hard lessons to learn, but she'd learned them well. And a thousand Lorne Quentins weren't going to make her forget.

Rachel began to eat her salad. It was no wonder, really, that she had been so stiff, so defensive, with Lorne since coming to work for him. Her determination not to let him get close to her caused her to clam up like an oyster when he was about. None of the other men affected her in the same way. With Mike, for instance, she was already on easy, almost affectionate terms. But then, Mike wasn't a threat. No warning bells clanged when he was around, and in any case, he was engaged to Lorne's secretary, Julie, who had also quickly become Rachel's friend, and neither of them had eyes for anyone but each other.

I don't know why I'm worrying, all the same, she thought ruefully. Lorne might attract her, but he showed no signs of feeling the same way towards her. Oh, he noticed her — noticed her clothes, her hair, her figure, she could tell that — but in a coolly impersonal way that Rachel perversely found annoying and made her dress with extra care, almost calling attention to the femininity he seemed determined not to acknowledge. Perhaps it was the way he expressed his prejudice, she thought with a touch of bitterness. Not that he'd ever admit it!

"Mind if I join you?"

Rachel looked up with a start that clattered her fork on her plate. Silvery grey eyes looked down at her; eyes that had only seconds ago haunted her mind. A tall, leanly-muscled body, outlined by the light suit he wore, loomed over her, long fingers resting lightly on the back of the chair opposite. The mouth was unsmiling, but one of the dark brows quirked in enquiry.

"Were you waiting for someone?"

"Oh — no, do sit down," Rachel said hurriedly, feeling her cheeks colour, and she picked up her fork with fingers that shook a little. "I'm sorry, you surprised me, I was miles away. I thought you were out today."

"I was. I got back earlier than I expected." He glanced briefly at the menu and gave the waitress his order. "I'm glad to have this chance to talk with you, Rachel. There was something I wanted to discuss."

"About work?" That was a silly question! What else could Lorne Quentin have to discuss with her?

"In a way. But not to do with *your* work." He hesitated, then as his meal arrived he waited until the waitress had gone. "It's about Arthur Morris — you know, the old man who's retiring soon? He's been with the firm ever since my grandfather started it and I want to give him something special in the way of a send-off. A party, of course, and a leaving present from the firm. I wondered if you might have any ideas."

Rachel looked at him in surprise. "Why me? I've only just come here. You must know Arthur well — or his workmates do — surely someone else would have a better idea of what he'd like than I would?"

"Oh yes, I know him well, and he's popular with the other men. But I'm looking for something a bit more original than the usual run of leaving presentations. Something that's unusual, yet exactly what the old man would like — something he'd never think of asking for himself. I thought you might have ideas that the rest of us wouldn't."

"I see. The woman's touch." Her tone was dry, and she saw Lorne make a tiny movement, quickly restrained.

"I suppose that's what I was thinking, yes," he agreed, his voice tight. "But perhaps you'd rather I didn't bother you with it. As you say, you hardly know Arthur, you can't really be interested."

"No," Rachel put out her own hand, palm upwards in a gesture of atonement, "I didn't mean that. Of course I'm interested — I think Arthur's a fine man, a real craftsman, he deserves to be shown appreciation. I take it you're thinking of something different from the traditional gold watch?"

"I certainly am! I've never understood why a watch has come to be the accepted mark of a man's retirement. Or a clock. Or a teamaker! The last thing you want to be reminded of in retirement, I'd have thought, is time, and as for an appliance that wakes you up with tea — well, it's when you're working you need that, not when you've given up!"

Rachel laughed. It was the most emphatic remark Lorne had made to her since she'd arrived; until now he'd seemed to be responding to her own stiffness with a cool formality of his own. But the moment didn't last. As their eyes met and she caught the flicker of warmth in his, her senses recoiled in alarm, and as if he'd seen it happen his own expression changed and he looked away.

"I'm sure you're right," Rachel said after a moment, laying her knife and fork neatly together. "So you want some other ideas." She thought for a moment, considering the possible desires of a man about to retire. "What about a holiday?"

"A holiday?"

"Mm. I may be wrong about Arthur, but I've got an idea he isn't all that keen on retirement. I've talked to him quite a bit, you know, and I think he's going to miss the factory — the cars and the companionship. Don't you think it might be a good idea to give him a really good break, get him away for a while so that he can get used to not having to come in every day?" A further thought struck her. "*I* know! At least — you might think it's going over the top a bit, it's probably much more than you'd meant — but what about Canada?"

"*Canada?*" Lorne stared at her as if she'd suddenly sprouted horns. "Why Canada, for heaven's sake?"

"His daughter lives there. She's got a baby, a granddaughter Arthur's never seen. And since he was widowed she's all the family he's got." Rachel leaned across the table, green eyes sparkling. "Don't you think it's a marvellous idea, Lorne? You'd only need to pay his fare, it probably wouldn't come to much more than the cost of a package holiday in Spain. And he'd certainly like it a lot better! What do you say?"

Lorne's eyes were still on her face, taking in every detail of her eager eyes, her softly-parted lips, the enthusiasm in her voice. Rachel watched him impatiently. What was the matter with the man, was he mesmerised? Probably he was wishing he'd never asked her — he couldn't have expected to spend so much on Arthur after all. The light began to die from her face, and Lorne spoke hastily.

"Yes, it's a great idea. I'm just astounded that you should come up with it so quickly. And how do you know all this about Arthur? *I* didn't know his daughter was in Canada, or that she had a baby."

"I told you, I've talked to him." She didn't tell him that in some queer way Arthur reminded her of her own grand-father, who had worked as a gamekeeper all his life and was, superficially, as different from Arthur as cheese was from coal-dust. All the same, there was the same attitude of pride in the job, of integrity and honest, earthy humility in both of them. She had recognised it on that first day, when Mike had shown her round the factory, and she'd made an opportunity several times since to talk with the old man. "Look, Arthur's the kind of man who doesn't ask much for himself. He could probably save up for his fare to Canada quite easily, but he'd be more likely to put the money in the bank to leave to his daughter when he dies, than to spend it going to see her. And he certainly wouldn't normally accept it as a present, or even a loan. But if you give it to him as his leaving present, well, then he'll accept it quite happily. A leaving present wouldn't hurt his pride, even if it is quite generous, especially as he's been here all his life."

Lorne gazed at her, his mind obviously turning over the possibilities of her idea. Rachel looked back thoughtfully. She knew that Mike Dalton had been right when he'd told her that Lorne cared about his employees and did his best to keep them happy. All the same, she was slightly surprised to find him prepared to take so much trouble over one man's retirement. And she wondered again, just as she had wondered several times in the past few weeks, just why Lorne had never married. Why his caring didn't operate on a more personal level; why it didn't deepen into loving.

"I thought I knew my employees pretty well," Lorne said at last, "but in a month you've found out more about the one who's been here the longest — a man I've known all my life — than I ever knew. You have considerable insight, Rachel."

"Well, it's for you to decide," Rachel said, feeling more uncomfortable under his approving scrutiny than when he looked at her coldly. "I'll try to think of some other ideas if you like."

"No, I think that one's fine. We'll have to work out the details, of course. For instance, do we stick out our necks and actually buy Arthur's ticket, or do we just give him a cheque and tell him that's what he's to do with it? And when should he go — immediately after retirement, or some time later? And there's his daughter, too . . ." Lorne was clearly finding that the solution to one problem invariably brought others in its train, and Rachel held up her hand.

"Stop it! Look, all that's easy enough to work out. Why don't you leave it to me? I can sound out Arthur, and he'll never know I'm doing it. Get Julie to arrange the party for you and I'll do the rest. That's if you'd like me to."

Lorne's eyes met hers across the table. They had darkened to a smoky grey, and she felt a quick twinge of response low in her stomach. "I'd like you to very much," he said quietly, and Rachel stared back at him, speechless and suddenly scared. The rest of the room seemed to fade and disappear; she was conscious only of Lorne, of his smoky eyes, of his long fingers lying so close to hers on the table.

She never knew, after that, whether she was relieved or sorry when the waitress materialised at their side, holding out her menu and asking if they wanted a dessert. Nor did she know what dessert it was that she chose, or what it tasted like.

All the same, she felt as they walked back to the offices together a short time later that they had somehow changed their footing for a more friendly one. The fact that Lorne had actually asked her advice was surely a good omen for the future. It meant that he was beginning to accept her as one of his team, that he was satisfied with her work and starting to think of her as a long-term associate, rather than someone there on approval.

And it meant that he was beginning to accept her on a more personal level; that he was beginning to like her.

It was oddly important, she realised, that he should like her. And that was something that had nothing to do with sexual attraction. With a quickening of surprise, she realised that it was because she liked him, because she would like to think they were friends. Nothing more than that, of course — just friends.

The only thing she wasn't sure about was whether Lorne was the kind of man a woman could be simply friends with. Hadn't she already decided that he was the kind of man who had affairs? Could he really be both?

No, it would be far, far better to keep things on a professional basis, Rachel decided. Easier to handle. Safer. And much, much more sensible.

"I'll come in for a moment," Lorne said as they reached her office door. "There's something about that design you submitted the other day — a few points I'd like to go over." He followed her into the large, airy office which had probably once been a morning-room, with tall French windows opening on to the sunny garden that was still kept up. Rachel went to a cabinet and took out the drawings while Lorne gazed absently at a huge bush of blazing scarlet rhododendrons that must have been there when he was a child. She laid the papers on her desk and he came over to look at them.

"Yes. Here and here." His tapering finger pointed. "I don't like that much — not racy enough. And the five-door concept gives the wrong image — too staid. In fact, the whole design is wrong. Two rows of seats, why, the thing looks like a mini-bus!"

"But I thought this was aimed at the young executive?" Rachel interrupted. "A status symbol for the up-and-coming whizz-kid."

"Exactly. A perk for the job — not a tool. This isn't for the rep or the consultant who may have to carry samples, displays, equipment of any sort. The whole idea of this car is to differentiate between that class of employee and the young manager, a man who's on his way up the ladder but not yet in the position of having a chauffeur-driven limo. The young chap in his thirties, late twenties even, who wants something to impress, both professionally and socially."

"Quite. So he's going to be visiting other firms, attending conferences and so on. But he's also going to be using his car privately as a family car. A man of that age is likely to have children, Lorne, young children who need ferrying about. He'll be taking them out and about at weekends, taking them on holiday. Have *you* ever tried packing two children and all their holiday gear into a two-door car with a rear that slopes down as much as you say this one should? Or jamming three or four boxes of assorted groceries into a boot that will hardly take a shopping-basket? Or lifting awkward items over the back of a front seat that has to be held forward with one knee while you struggle? This design just isn't practical as you want it, not for what you want it for."

"The young executive I'm thinking of," Lorne said, "will be able to afford to buy his wife her own car for shopping and ferrying children."

"And is that going to be the car he wants to use at weekends or to go on holiday in?" Rachel demanded. "Think again, Lorne. Most second cars — and it's always the wife's that's the 'second' one, with all that implies — are smaller, older and less reliable. Even if they're new, they're never bigger and better than the car the husband drives to work and probably leaves in a car park all day. I tell you, if an executive such as you describe is supplied with this car, it won't be impressing anyone at all at weekends or during holiday times. It'll be at home in the garage while the 'second' car is out and about. And your high-flying whizz-kid isn't going to want to use an old banger, or even a new compact then. He'll want to keep up his image. He'll have to spend more money than he wants on that 'second' car, buying something that will continue to display his status. He isn't going to like you for that, Lorne." She paused. "He isn't going to want your racy little number at all. He's going to ask his firm for something a bit more functional."

She held Lorne's gaze coolly. Talking to him like this, on a level at which she felt confident, her jumpy awareness of him vanished. They were no longer man and woman, circling each other as warily as two wild animals. She was a professional, talking a language they both understood, and she could see that he was listening to her on the same level — or almost. He still wasn't, she thought, quite as ready to

69

accept her views as he would have been if they had come from a man.

"So what are you suggesting?" he said finally. "A sit-up-and-beg family saloon of the old school?"

Rachel moved impatiently. "I've never suggested anything of the kind. What we're talking now is people-carriers. That's the latest name for them now." She looked up at him incredulously. "Don't tell me you've not noticed them, Lorne! Where have you been living? You're a car designer, you ought to know *exactly* what your rivals are doing, you ought to *know* what's on the road —"

"And so I do," he interrupted, his eyes darkening with annoyance. "You don't have to talk as if I'm some kind of dinosaur, Rachel. But Quentin's have always been a very individual car, and I see no cause to follow the fashion of the time simply to keep up with my 'rivals'." He paused. "In fact, I don't concede that Quentin's *has* any rivals. We're just not part of the general run of car manufacture."

Rachel shrugged. "That's fair enough. I don't have any quarrel with that. But in that case, you shouldn't be thinking of making cars for companies to give their

70

executives. You should stick to your racy, individual cars and flip your fingers at the customers who have their own requirements. Take it or leave it — isn't that what you're saying?"

"Put crudely, I suppose it is," he snapped. "And it's always worked for us in the past. People have been glad to buy our cars on our terms, and still will, I haven't the slightest doubt."

"So why in heaven's name are you even considering this?" Rachel stabbed at the designs with one index finger. "You're trying to keep a foot in both camps, Lorne, and it just won't work."

He sighed. "Do I have to spell it out for you? Economics, Rachel. We need another line —"

"So the individual car isn't working? Or at least, not well enough to keep the factory going all on its own."

He bit his lip, looking angry. Rachel watched him, knowing that there was a struggle going on behind that proud forehead. Perhaps I've been too harsh, she thought. It can't be easy to have to compromise. For a moment, she wanted to comfort him, to soften her words, but then she straightened her own shoulders. Lorne was a grown man, not a baby. He didn't need mothering, and he was strong enough to face unpalatable truths.

"You don't believe in pulling your punches, do you, Rachel?" he said at last. "All right, if that's the way you want to put it —"

"Don't try to blame me for telling the truth," she cut in. "It's not my responsibility to decide on your policies. It isn't the way I *want* to put it — it's just the way it seems to me. You can accept it or not, just as you wish."

Lorne sighed. "All right. You've made your point." He looked down at the design again. "And yes, on balance, I do want to have this contract. But I still want the car to be individual — to carry the Quentin stamp."

"And so it can," Rachel said eagerly. "Look, there's nothing to be ashamed of in making a people-carrier, Lorne. They're taking over in the middle-market — the people who can't quite make it to Range Rover but want something more than an ordinary estate. Why, even the Prime Minister's using one! You can't get more upmarket than that. And we can give our people-carrier the Quentin touch, which nobody else can do." Her slender forefinger moved across the design, indicating what she meant. "Look here, and here. Isn't that streamlined enough? Isn't this advanced? Don't you think a young executive — who's still, admittedly, hankering after the racy sports model of his single days — will like this feature? I've thought about these things, Lorne, but I've also projected my thoughts to look at the other parts of his life. He isn't just an executive, you see, he's other things as well — husband, father, son. And those things will affect the car he likes to drive and, therefore, us." She gave him a quick, slanting glance, green eyes wide and innocent. "Isn't that what you wanted?"

Lorne's eyes were as dark as winter clouds, a hint of a storm somewhere in their depths, and Rachel suddenly lost the feeling of protection against his masculinity that their impersonal talk about design had given her. Abruptly, she was aware of just how close they were standing; of Lorne's hand, still resting in the drawing, uncomfortably near to her own pointing finger; of his breath, warm on her cheek. Of the fact — the inescapable fact — that they were a man and a woman, and all alone.

Jerkily, she moved away, her cheeks warmed now by more than his breath. She fought to keep her voice cool, saying quickly: "Well, wasn't it? Don't you agree with me?"

Lorne never took his eyes from her face. She could feel their glance like a razor, slicing through her mind, reading the confused tangle of thoughts and making some kind of sense from them. If only she could turn off that almost tangible, *sensual* force that emanated from him. Did he do it deliberately, or was it something he just couldn't help?

Lorne spoke at last, but his voice was distracted, as if while answering her question he was really answering something else, something neither of them had put into words. "I'm not sure," he said vaguely, and Rachel gave him a quick, surprised look; she had never associated Lorne with vagueness before. "I'll have to think about it again. There are points I haven't considered before."

"Quite." Rachel pulled herself together, aware that the conversation could easily slip away from her. Lorne seemed to be talking about something entirely different, and she had to keep it on a track she could control. "You've looked at it only from the point of the executive as an executive — a work-machine. But he's a man too, a man with a background, with family life, other interests and needs." She almost faltered as she caught Lorne's gaze on her again, unfathomable, intent. What was he making of her words now, for heaven's sake? "Those are what you hadn't considered," she went on determinedly, "and they're what will sell this car for you — or not. Your top manager isn't the same. He doesn't mind his car being suitable only for his working day. A big, luxury limousine is just what he needs for his successful image. He wouldn't want to use it for the family — except perhaps for visiting his son at school — but that doesn't matter, he can afford to buy whatever he wants for private use, and for his wife too. He's into the second and third car bracket. But the up-and-coming executive is different. Every penny he spends has got to work for him. His house, his family, his whole lifestyle. His car." She paused, more confident again now, feeling that she'd skated successfully over that dangerous patch, that they were back on firm ground. "He doesn't want to spend unnecessarily on that second car. He's got too many other expenses."

"You don't sound as if you like either of them very much," Lorne observed, and

Rachel shrugged.

"That doesn't really come into it, does it? All right, that kind of lifestyle wouldn't be my choice — acquiring status symbols and keeping up with the Jones's doesn't interest me. But I'm not here to impose my preferences on others. I'm here to design the cars they want, and I believe I *know* what they want — in this case, anyway."

"It's odd," Lorne said as if following his own line of thought, his eyes still on hers in that disconcerting manner that seemed to imply he knew more about what was going on inside her head than she did herself. "I'd have said that in describing the rising young executive and his lifestyle, you were describing exactly the lifestyle you'd want for yourself. Except for the family, of course — you don't qualify there." He didn't seem to notice Rachel's quick spasm of pain. "But in everything else — the image of the determined, reach-for-the-sky high achiever — well, it's you right down to the ground."

There was a moment of stillness, then Rachel said quietly: "Was that intended to be offensive?"

Lorne's eyes widened, and now their darkness had cleared and they were the innocent, pearly grey of a summer dawn.

"Offensive? In what way?"

"You speak as if family life were something I'd never 'qualify' for," she said, unable to keep an edge of bitterness from her voice.

"I'm sorry. I certainly never intended it to sound like that. I simply took it for granted that it was something you'd discounted in your scheme of things. You seem so determined to make it in car design, and I've no doubt at all that with your abilities and dedication you'll do so. I can't imagine that you'll ever let such distractions as love and marriage come between you and your ambition."

Rachel looked at him. Was he being deliberately provocative, saying things that attacked her womanhood in the hope of getting her to rise to the bait? He'd said something similar before, she remembered, at her interview, when he'd observed that ambition was 'unfeminine'.

"And do you believe that love and marriage would automatically make me a less good designer?" she enquired. "Do you believe it would be impossible for me to give my mind to work if I were constantly worrying about what to cook for my lord and master's supper? Or are you just afraid that I'll fall in love with someone as old-fashioned as yourself, who'd want me to give up my job and stay at home with a pramful of babies? And you'd have to go through all the business of appointing an Assistant Designer, all over again?"

Lorne laughed. "Nothing of the sort. Haven't I just said that I can't imagine you ever allowing such a thing to happen? No, I think you'll be with us for quite a long time, Rachel. As long as it suits you, anyway. I don't imagine we'll be discussing *your* retirement party in thirty years or so's time. By then, you'll have picked a much juicier plum for yourself, and all credit to you if you do."

"In other words, as you said before, I'm too ambitious to be feminine." Her eyes were darting green fire at him, but he appeared not to notice.

"On the contrary," he drawled, and let his eyes move slowly over her figure, outlined in a slim green and white linen dress, its scoop neck revealing skin already lightly tanned by early summer sun. She stood quite still under his gaze, thankful that he couldn't see the sudden rapid beating of her heart against her ribs, but unable to prevent the rise of colour in her cheeks under his scrutiny. How had the conversation got back to this, she wondered, when she'd been so sure she had control of it? She saw the twitch of his mouth as he noted her blush then felt the colour deepen as his glance settled on her full lower lip, caught between small white teeth.

"On the contrary," he repeated, and there was a note of amusement in his voice, "I'd say that in some ways you're very feminine indeed."

"Oh, for goodness' sake!" Rachel snapped, turning away. "Why do men always have to reduce things to a *physical* level? Why can't they — why can't *you* — ever forget I'm a woman? Why does it have to *matter* so much?"

"Why indeed?" She was startled by a new harshness in Lorne's tone, but before she could react he had stepped forward and caught her by the shoulders, twisting her to face him. Rachel drew a quick, indignant breath but as she stared up at him her protest died in her throat. "Why *does* it matter so much?" he repeated, his eyes stormy with anger now. "Why does it matter so much to *you?* Because you're the one who keeps calling attention to your sex, Rachel, or hadn't you realised that? Hadn't you realised that it seems to be on your mind practically all the time? Maybe not. Maybe you hadn't realised, either, that you go out of your way to *tell* everyone you're a woman — just in case they couldn't see it for themselves. Maybe you haven't realised that you dress in ways that will emphasise it, make it impossible for a man to forget . . ." Keeping his hands on her shoulder, he traced his thumbs along the neckline of her dress, following the edge of the material to the sensitive area just above the cleft of her breasts. "These clothes you wear — skirts that fit your neat little bottom like a skin, shirts and blouses that stop just short of indecency — all in the best possible taste, I agree, but then you've got the money to buy quality, haven't you? If one of the typists tried to dress like you on her wage, she'd simply end up looking tarty. But you, you've got the looks, the figure, the taste to know just how far you can go and get away with it. And don't you just take advantage of those qualities!"

Rachel stood under his hands, feeling whipped by the lash of his words. Was it true — was that really how he saw her? As no more than a tease, a woman who promised all and gave nothing, flaunted her body but kept it firmly out of reach? Well, he certainly wasn't reading her mind now!

Didn't he have any idea at all what his touch was doing to her? His fingers were burning brands on her shoulders, searing fire down through her body. She was sharply aware of every one of his contours, a tantalising inch or so away from hers. For a mad, dizzy moment, she had an impulse to step forward, to sway just that inch necessary, to press herself against that hard body, to lift her face to his . . .

With an effort that took more strength than she knew she had, she thrust the image away. Wasn't that just what Lorne would delight in — knowing that his sheer masculinity could overwhelm her, make her his slave? Knowing that, in the end, she hadn't been able to resist him? All right, she was a woman, she could feel that dangerous power of his — she could *enjoy* it, if she wanted to. But it couldn't be allowed to happen just because *he* wanted it. The choice had to be hers.

And she chose no.

"I told you," she said through her teeth, "I don't deny my sex. I see no reason why I should. You dress like a man. I dress like a woman. I enjoy wearing the clothes I think suit me. That's all there is to it."

"Not quite all," he said softly, his thumbs still caressing her neck in that disturbing, distracting way. "Because you want to have it both ways, don't you, Rachel, my dear. You want to acknowledge your own femininity — you want to emphasise it. And you want me to acknowledge it too. It annoys you almost beyond toleration when I don't — doesn't it?" His thumbs pressed on a sensitive spot and Rachel gasped. She wanted to protest, to twist out of his arms, to make some violent response, but she couldn't move. And Lorne was speaking again, his tones cool, level, as if he were explaining some point she hadn't quite understood. "You want me to treat you like a man and admire you as a woman. You want the respect I'd give to a man — which I'm quite ready to give you in those areas in which you earn it — but you don't want it to end there. You want the other kinds of treatment, that I certainly would *not* give to a man — the kinds I'd accord a beautiful woman who was just and only that. In fact, you want it all. You say you want equality. I think you are looking for idolatry."

"You *do?*" Rachel was fighting for composure now. She was receiving so many messages, from both Lorne and her own mind, instincts and reason, that she didn't know where to begin to sort them out. His hands were fire on her shoulders, kneading the soft flesh gently, the way a cat kneads a lap before it settles down — with a hint of claws that could grip at the first unwelcome movement. His body was far too close now, and if she trembled any more he would be able to feel her involuntary movements against him. Against him . . . she quivered at the thought. She'd chosen no. *She'd chosen no.*

She concentrated on his words, those hurtful, insulting words. They were like thongs, lashing into her feelings, curdling a bruised indignation that stung her eyes with angry tears. How *dare* he suggest that she was using her body to exact special treatment? Because that's what he *was* saying, wasn't it? That she wanted special treatment, admiration, for being a woman, for being attractive and not being ashamed of it? How *dare* he?

"Forget you're a woman?" Lorne said, and his voice was harsh, ragged, his fingers savage on her tender flesh. "I only wish I could! I only wish you'd give me the chance!"

He jerked her against him with a hungry ferocity that took her completely by surprise, his mouth meeting hers with such force that she felt the clash of his teeth against her own. His tongue was like a thrusting invader, forcing its way past her parted lips, darting into the soft recesses of her mouth, demanding, insistent, irresistible. With a last shred of horror that was only a fraction of the whirling confusion of sensation that had suddenly become her world, Rachel found herself responding, letting her lips part more readily, letting her body soften against him, moulding to his shape as his hands slipped down from her shoulders and circled over her back, one coming to rest on her slender waist while the other splayed itself over what he had only just described as her 'neat little bottom' . . .

Rachel caught at the memory of those words, struggling for the indignation they had provoked in her. But it didn't seem to matter any more that she'd found them insulting, that she'd raged inwardly against every word that Lorne had spoken. Nothing mattered but this — the feel of his hard body against hers, the aroused virility that spoke so clearly to her own starving instincts, crying out for the feeding of a hunger she'd repressed for so long. Yearnings she'd ignored for years burst from some hidden place like the waters of a shattered dam, desires that had been damped down only to smoulder danger-ously beneath the surface, flared up and threatened to explode. All reason gone, she groaned and clung to Lorne as if to a life-line, returning kiss for kiss, moving her body sensuously against him, letting her own hands begin a journey of exploration as intimate as his. Joyously, her tongue met his to caress it with a sensuality that dragged a low groan from deep in his throat; excitement scorched along her veins, burning into her mind, shutting out with flames of passion the existence of any-thing but this moment, of herself and Lorne, of a need that had to be fulfilled.

Four

The sudden scream of her telephone wrenched at her brain. It seemed to rip the world wide open. Almost before Rachel was aware of hearing it, she and Lorne had torn themselves apart and were staring at each other in shocked disbelief.

The telephone rang again, sharply, insistently. It was a demanding instrument, Rachel had always thought — wonderful because she could pick it up, dial a number and miraculously be talking to her brother in Australia. But tyrannical because it always demanded — and got — attention, in the office, when you were working; in shops, being served or waiting in a queue. The telephone had only to ring once for every other task to be dropped immediately in order to answer its shrill call.

Now, it had cut into a scene that could — would? — change Rachel's entire life, sharply reminding her of the existence of that other world, the one she lived and moved in every day, the one that depended on her retaining that detached independence that was essential for her survival. She put a shaking hand to her head. How near had she been to throwing away everything she had worked towards, built up during the past few years? How close had she come to submission, to letting a man into her heart, to allowing Lorne Quentin of all people to take her over, dominate her in that way that could mean only one thing — death to her personality, her identity?

The telephone rang for the third time, and Rachel walked across to her desk, conscious of trembling legs and wondering if her voice would give her away. Did Penny know Lorne was in here with her? She picked up the receiver.

"Sorry to bother you when it's still your lunch-hour," Penny's young voice said, "but it's the estate agent. He's got a cottage he thinks you might be interested in. He wants you to see it as soon as possible." Her voice was apologetic as she added: "I wouldn't have disturbed you, but I know you're keen to find somewhere."

"Oh — yes. Thank you. Put him through, will you?" Rachel still wasn't in full command of her senses and the abrupt change of emotion in the past few minutes had left her feeling sick and dizzy, but at least she was beginning to realise what had happened — what had almost happened — and to feel grateful to the estate agent, to Penny, to the telephone itself for slicing into the moment. She waited for the estate agent to come through and felt her mind twist with agony. How *could* she have let it happen, for God's sake? She'd *known*, known just what effect Lorne could have on her, known just how she must react if he touched her, kissed her. Had she *wanted* it? Uncomfortably, she had to admit that a part of her must have done — that dark, hidden part that she liked to think she had under control these days. But that wasn't the part that she wanted to govern her life, any more than she wanted Lorne governing her life — as he would, one way or another, if she gave way to him now.

She heard the estate agent's voice and at the same time she turned to see what Lorne was doing, to make sure that he was keeping his distance. If he came over and touched her now . . . But he was at the other side of the room, sitting in an armchair that was drawn up beside the French window. He was half turned away from her, looking out, the lines of his body tense. She could see that his eyes were narrowed, as if in deep thought. Well, of course he was thinking! Thinking that he'd

88

been right about her, that she was nothing but a scheming tart, that he'd made a big mistake in appointing her, that all his prejudices were right — women were nothing but trouble, that he should never have bowed to the modern trend for them to have careers; that, as soon as possible, he would find some excuse for getting rid of her.

Rachel's mind seemed to be split in two as she talked with the estate agent on one level, taking details of the cottage, making an appointment to go and see it, while at a deeper, more fundamental level she was still arguing mentally with Lorne. All right, so he believed she'd given him provocation, but he hadn't *had* to kiss her, had he? He hadn't had to give way to his own desires — his *lusts* — like that. There'd been something almost animal in the way he'd pulled her against him, taken her mouth, caressed her body. It didn't help that Rachel knew she'd responded in exactly the same instinctive way. It made her all the angrier. Angry that he should have been able to provoke such a response, ashamed that she hadn't been able to resist it, followed by an increased surge of anger. She didn't *want* to feel shame — she didn't like it, not a bit.

She put down the phone at last, and

Lorne turned back to her, his expression telling her nothing. If he felt anything at all now, he wasn't going to let it show; maybe he was waiting for her to make the first move. Well, in that case he'd have to wait. They watched each other warily, tension cracking the air between them.

"I suppose you'd like me to apologise," Lorne said at last, stiffly.

"Don't you think you should?"

He shrugged his big shoulders. "Not entirely. I had both provocation —" she'd known he would say *that*, "— and co-operation. I can see from your face, however, that you don't agree."

"I certainly don't. It's the old cop-out, isn't it? It's trotted out in most rape cases, I believe. A girl dresses attractively so she's 'asking for it'. She goes out on a date so she's offering herself. She's walking along a lonely road because that's where she lives, yet she can't blame a man if he attacks her — she should have expected it. The woman gets the blame for the man's baser instincts all the time. There's never any hint that the man could just possibly control those instincts."

"Oh, come now," Lorne said with a mildness she didn't believe in for a moment, "don't you think you're overstating the case? You can't deny that you did provoke me. And you certainly can't deny that you co-operated — there was no suggestion of attempted rape there, you were most enthusiastic. Quite took me by surprise."

Rachel bit her lip. This was an argument she couldn't win, she knew that. Because he was right — she couldn't deny her response. That didn't mean she had to be proud of it, though, or want to repeat it.

She looked at Lorne in silence, weighing up what was the best answer. Maidenly protests would be dismissed as both coy and unrealistic, and she had to admit he'd be right. He saw her as a mature, experienced woman who had returned his advance with interest. That wasn't quite the truth, but there was no way of convincing him — not without telling him a lot more about herself than she wanted to. The best approach, she thought, would be a down-to-earth one, keeping it all on a purely physical level, cutting emotion right out.

"All right, so I quite enjoyed it," she said coolly, proud of that 'quite'. If it gave Lorne the impression that she'd had more lovers than hot dinners, that couldn't be helped. "But you have to realise that such

91

a response is a purely animal thing. You took me rather by surprise, that's all, and you're obviously quite experienced." Another nice 'quite'. She was beginning to regain her confidence now, to feel back in command of herself. "It didn't mean anything, and it won't happen again — forewarned is forearmed." She gave him a steady look. "I mean it when I say it won't happen again, Lorne. We work together and I don't think it's a good idea to mix business and pleasure."

His eyes glinted. "So you admit it was a pleasure?" he murmured, and Rachel lowered her eyes so that he wouldn't see the effect his silky tones had on her. "All right, Rachel. In the interests of Quentin Motors we'll consider the incident over and forgotten." A silvery gleam as he added: "Well, perhaps not entirely forgotten. The memory can linger on . . . And I'm afraid I can't share your optimism — if that's the right word — that it won't happen again. I happen to have a healthy respect for human desires — or, as you'd probably prefer to call them, animal lusts. I think they have a way of getting there in the end. But time will tell."

He got up and stretched, and Rachel had a brief memory of that taut, muscular body against hers before she turned away, determined not to let her awareness of him have its way again. She'd meant it when she told Lorne she didn't want to mix business with pleasure; she'd done it once, with disastrous results. It wasn't a risk she was likely to repeat.

"I'll get on with these designs," she said tightly, going back to the desk where they lay. "I'll let you have them when I've finished."

Lorne said nothing; and when she turned back at last, the room was empty.

Rachel did her best, during the next few weeks, to settle in at Quentin Motors. In any other circumstances, she reflected bitterly, it would have been easy. She worked well with Mike and the rest of the team. She found the work challenging, stretching her skills as they had never been stretched at Britton Cars, and thus more satisfying when she came up with the solution to a difficult problem or an innovative idea. She loved the small cottage she had bought, its solitude in the peaceful countryside, and enjoyed working in such beautiful surroundings. But none of it could compensate for the tension that gripped her whenever she came into contact with — or even thought about — Lorne Quentin.

It didn't even seem to help that she could find a hundred and one ways of avoiding him. Most of her work was done with Mike, and she could often make some excuse not to see Lorne, leaving Mike to go over any points with him that needed to be discussed — Mike was, after all, Chief Designer. She grew to know just when Lorne might be expected in the office, when he was likely to arrive and depart, and she could time her own arrivals and departures accordingly. It was almost as if she had grown extra-sensitive antennae where he was concerned. And she suspected once or twice that Lorne himself was actively co-operating in this evasion of hers, never coming into her office alone, rarely staying longer than was absolutely necessary and barely glancing at her while he was there.

She supposed she ought to be glad about that but, perversely, she found herself resenting it, feeling angry and hurt when he had passed her by with little more than a 'good-morning', feeling squashed and humiliated when he came into the drawing-office with Mike and gave her a mere cursory nod before continuing with what he was saying. If he'd been trying to humiliate her, he was going just the right way about it. But she had to admit that she had, quite literally, asked for it. And once she'd sorted out her feelings, she would surely be grateful for it. All the same . . .

Too often, Rachel found her mind going back to that afternoon, when Lorne Quentin had held her in his arms and kissed her. She still found herself growing hot when she remembered it, a tingling sensation spreading through her body as she recalled the kisses that had touched a spring in her emotions, acting like tinder to a fire that had been dormant. She shivered as she felt again those strong hands, with their long fingers, moving over her body, and turned her head restlessly on her pillow at night when her dreams allowed them to roam further and more intimately. She was shocked by the way her thoughts lingered on Lorne Quentin's lean face, his taut body, the loose-limbed grace of his movements. And she was angered by the way her heart jerked whenever she saw him, the way her breathing suddenly became difficult and her face grew warm with colour. Damn the man she thought viciously. Why did he have to have this effect on her? Why couldn't he have been old, middle-aged, unprepossessing, dull?

Or just safely married, absorbed in a wife and family so that he didn't need to put out this almost tangible aura of sexual attraction?

She didn't allow herself to analyse why the thought of Lorne married gave her heart an unexpected twist of pain.

"Oh, there you are," Mike Dalton said, greeting her as she came into the main drawing-office. "Look, Lorne's called a special meeting for ten o'clock. Some new order that's come in. Can you get clear in time?"

"It's not really a question of whether I *can*, surely," Rachel said wryly. "When Lorne calls a special meeting, we *all* get cleared up in time . . . Yes, of course I'll be there. What is this new order? Sounds exciting."

"He'll tell you then. I've got to rush now — see you later." Mike gave her a quick grin and departed, leaving Rachel curious and amused. Lorne had evidently sworn Mike to secrecy, preferring to give them the news himself. She went through to her own office and settled down to work, wondering idly what the new order might be. Orders for Quentin cars were coming in all the time, and because all the cars were custom-built they took a long time to fulfil.

Any order coming in today might be several years in execution, but the people who bought Quentin cars were aware of that, and prepared to wait.

It seemed at first that this was just another order which required particular attention, but as the meeting in Lorne's office progressed, Rachel began to realise that about this one there was something extra-special. The customer was a big property magnate and he wanted a small fleet of cars for his top executives, men whose own names were nationally-known. And this was a customer who wasn't prepared to wait for several years — he wanted his fleet within twelve months.

"We can use the new design we've been working on, with certain modifications," Lorne told the meeting. "But it means putting back some of our other work, and that's something we've never done before. We could take on extra staff, of course — in fact, we'll have to — but the really important work has to be done by our own craftsmen, the ones who have been working on Quentin cars for years. And the same goes for all our other orders, of course, I'm not intending to sell anyone short."

"You will be, though, won't you?" Rachel

said, knowing that several of the men were turning to look at her in surprise. "If you put back other orders. I don't see how you can do otherwise."

"That's what we're here to discuss," Lorne told her, and she immediately felt humiliated. She bit her lip and remained silent as the discussion began, listening as various members put forward their views and suggestions. She had to admit that they were mostly sensible ones, and that everyone was clearly anxious not to accept this quite valuable order at the expense of customers already on their books. At the same time, nobody wanted to lose it — the very fact that Quentin cars would be associated with the property firm would in itself be excellent advertising.

"Well, that seems to be all we can do for this morning," Lorne said at last. "I'm going to see Garfield Holt this afternoon and have some further talks with him. We'll have another meeting soon." He glanced up as chairs began to scrape back and people move about. "Don't go for a minute, will you, Rachel?"

Rachel, in the act of picking up her briefcase, stopped and stared at him, wondering why he wanted her to stay behind. Was he going to tell her that he'd decided against keeping her on? Her heart sank. In spite of the confusion of her feelings about him, she wanted desperately to stay with Quentin Motors. And she was sure that her work so far had been good. In any case, he would scarcely have asked her to attend the meeting if he'd been about to fire her.

The room cleared, leaving her alone with Lorne. She watched him warily and made sure that she was between him and the door — not that she expected him to make any passes here, at this time of the morning, with Julie liable to come in at any moment. But with a man like Lorne, clearly pleasurably aware of his own animal magnetism, you couldn't be too careful. It irritated her to see his finely-chiselled lips twitch and know that he was well aware of the thoughts passing through her mind.

"Well?" she said, more sharply than she intended. "I take it you've got something important to say to me?"

"Do you?" he returned, lazily. "I wonder why. Couldn't it just be that I'd like your company over coffee?"

Rachel sighed. "It seems unlikely," she said coolly. "We're both busy, aren't we? And we *are* here to work, not socialise."

"True, true. Perhaps we ought to do

something about that." His eyes glinted. "Have an evening out sometime — dinner, perhaps, or a concert. They have some very good ones in Birmingham, and it's not more than an hour's run away. Without any strings, of course. What do you think?"

"I'm not sure when I'll be free," Rachel said shortly, pausing as Julie brought in a tray of coffee and set it on the table. "Lorne, I really do have work to do — something I want to get finished today. So if you wouldn't mind telling me what it is you want? I'm sure it *isn't* my company, whatever you say!"

"Well, we won't argue over that." Lorne poured coffee into bone china cups and handed her one. "And as for the work you want to get finished — I'm afraid it will have to wait. I want you to come out with me this afternoon."

"Come out with you?" Rachel stared at him. "Out where? Why?"

"Oh, it's all right, I'm not suggesting anything illicit." Lorne's lips twitched again. "You really are very sensitive, Rachel. No, this is a perfectly proper business trip. I've an appointment with Garfield Holt this afternoon, as I've already said, and I want you to be there. There are certain design aspects we need to discuss and it seems only sensible to have the designer involved on the spot right from the start."

Rachel passed a hand across her forehead. She had a dizzy feeling that events were moving too fast. "You mean, you want *me* to work on the designs?" she asked blankly. "But we don't even agree on them ourselves, we argued over them before —" she stopped and bit her lip.

"Before the little episode we don't refer to, yes," Lorne cut in smoothly. "But we haven't discussed them since, have we? I've considered the points you made and although I don't entirely agree, I find some of them quite valid. And yes, I *do* want you to work primarily on this project. Holt has some quite specific requirements and I think your line of thought will match them rather well. That's why it's important for you to meet him as soon as possible."

"I see." Rachel was beginning slowly to assimilate the new situation. Most important of all was the fact that Lorne had evidently decided she was the right person for Quentin Motors — it blazed in her mind like the white light of tropical sunshine. Following it, came the growing excitement of a new car — a car that might become as

101

famous as the Britton Beagle, with all the added charisma of being not only a Quentin but a Quentin designed specifically for an internationally-known tycoon. She drank her coffee automatically, without noticing the taste.

"So you'll be ready immediately after lunch?" Lorne continued as if not noticing her reaction. "It's only an hour's drive from here to Holt's home — he lives in the Cotswolds. Should be quite a pleasant trip. We might have dinner on the way back, perhaps."

"Yes." Rachel was almost too dazed still to realise just what was happening. "I think I'd better go home and change before we leave," she said, looking down at her plain working dress. Since the 'episode' Lorne had referred to so sardonically, she'd taken to wearing demure, high-necked dresses, unaware of the fact that by contrast they made her striking looks all the more provocative. To her mind, the effect was merely drab. "I hadn't anticipated seeing anyone today."

"Fine. You slip back at lunchtime and I'll pick you up just before two." Lorne's manner had become brisk. "I'll have all the relevant details — there's nothing you need bring at this stage, other than a fresh notebook to jot down any ideas that might occur." He stood up and gave Rachel a friendly nod. "Let's wish this new venture all success, Rachel. I'm sure you're as keen as I am on that."

"Yes," Rachel said faintly, "let's."

She left the office, thankful for once that Julie wasn't in the outer office as she passed through. She needed time to take in this new development, time to prepare herself for this afternoon's trip. Not that she was worried about meeting Garfield Holt, she was quite confident of her ability to handle that. But the drive there and back with Lorne — and the possibility of dinner on the return journey — were factors that already had her shaking inside. She scolded herself, pointing out severely that Lorne had behaved impeccably over the past two or three weeks, making no effort to put her into a compromising position, treating her — even if she had, perversely, resented it — exactly as she had told him she wished to be treated, as a colleague, with sex playing no part in their relationship. And this morning he had been almost likeable — brisk and polite without being distant, a disarming friendliness creeping into his voice and manner as he talked. If he'd been like that to begin with, she thought wistfully, things might have been different. And then she caught herself up sharply. This way, she knew the real Lorne Quentin — this way, she was protected. However pleasant and friendly Lorne set out to be, he could never fool her now; never again take her by surprise.

She left early to go back to the cottage for a hasty lunch, delighting once again on the home she had found. It was completely different from her city flat, yet it seemed to complement her personality even more. Despite her haste, she paused for a moment as she opened the door, letting the peaceful atmosphere soak into her mind.

The cottage had once been two, lived in by farm workers. They had been knocked together long enough ago for the changes to be almost imperceptible, a part now of the charm. Like so many buildings in this part of the world, the cottages had been built with exposed beams both outside and in, and the walls had been limewashed in white. Inside, the main room still had one of the big inglenook fireplaces with an oven set into the side, and huge slabs of rock forming the lintel and part of the wall.

Rachel had spent a good deal of her

spare time in redecorating and arranging the cottage to her own satisfaction. Her bedroom, which had been rather shabby, was now fresh and pretty, papered in a design with tiny blue flowers scattered over it. She had added curtains with the same design, framing a view of the Black Mountains seen across the leafy Herefordshire landscape, and for the bed she had found a duvet cover and pillowslips in the same blue, with white flowers reversing the design. A white sheepskin rug on the blue carpet added a touch of luxury, and a few burgundy cushions on the wicker armchairs by the window brought the room a contrasting warmth.

In the bathroom, Rachel had wrought greater changes. That too had been rather shabby, so before moving in she had had the old suite taken out and replaced by pure white. There had been room to enlarge, and she now had a surprisingly spacious room, with a corner bath and a separate shower cubicle. The carpet here was burgundy, picking up its tone from the bedroom cushions, and she had found a few Italian tiles in burgundy and gold which, scattered at random over the gleaming white walls, added a touch of discreet opulence. The rest of the room's character came from Rachel's collection of cranberry glass which glowed from glass shelves on the window, and two or three pictures which she had backed in the same colour before framing.

As she moved swiftly from room to room, preparing for the afternoon, Rachel absorbed the impressions that the rooms never failed to give her. A sense of peace and tranquillity in her home was, she had found, vital to her wellbeing, and she had taken care to achieve it. But she had not forgotten the cottage's own character. The kitchen was traditionally country-style, with light oak fittings and a cluster of herbs on the wide windowsill. A scrubbed pine table stood at one end of the long room, and the Welsh dresser was ablaze with sunshine-yellow cups and saucers. It only wants a cat, curled up in a basket, to complete the picture, Rachel thought as she boiled an egg, and she made up her mind to look for a kitten as soon as possible.

As soon as she had eaten her snack, she showered and slipped into a pale green silk suit that looked both businesslike and feminine, contrasting subtly with her tawny hair and accentuating the colour of her eyes. It had grown warm during the morning, and she swept her hair up away from her neck into a loose knot that allowed curly tendrils to fall around her face, softening any severity that might have resulted. By the time she had slid her feet into strappy sandals that exactly matched the green of her suit, Lorne's car was drawing up at the cottage gate.

Rachel hastened downstairs but he was already inside when she reached the foot of the narrow stairs, looking around him with interest and approval. He gave her a quick, comprehensive glance and immediately she wondered if she were over-dressed.

"Nice little place," he remarked conversationally. "And quite a pleasant setting too."

"Yes, I think I was lucky to find it," Rachel answered shortly. For some reason she didn't care to analyse, she didn't want Lorne Quentin in her cottage a moment longer than was necessary. "I'm ready — shall we go?"

His dark eyebrows rose a fraction. "Sure. You're very punctual —"

"For a woman," Rachel supplied sardonically as he hesitated.

"I wasn't actually going to say that. But since you mention it, yes. I'm quite accustomed to being kept waiting by beautiful women."

"But that, presumably, is for pleasure. This is business."

"You mean," he said as she held the door for him to go out, "if I were taking you out for the evening, for pleasure, you'd keep me waiting too?"

"That's something we'll never know, isn't it?" Rachel said sweetly, and she locked the door behind them.

Lorne's car was the most de luxe of the Quentin range, a long, low monster with aggressive acceleration, and it surged along like a tidal wave. It could have been terrifying in the hands of the wrong driver, Rachel thought as they swept along the quiet roads, but she had to admit that Lorne's driving was immaculate — smooth, efficient, considerate of both car and passenger. The countryside slid past effortlessly, and roads which Rachel knew to be rough and bumpy suddenly seemed smooth and even.

After a while, Lorne began to talk easily, telling her about the places they were passing through, and in spite of herself Rachel found herself interested, enjoying his commentary. He pointed out the Malvern Hills, lying like a stranded whale on the horizon. When they crossed them she was surprised at the definite geological boundary they formed, leaving the rolling hills of Herefordshire behind them with the flat, chessboard plains of Worcestershire ahead. Only Bredon Hill broke the monotony, with the blue shadows of the Cotswolds rising in the distance. Rachel thought of Housman's poem about summertime on Bredon, and almost as if he had read her mind Lorne quoted the very words that were in her mind. "He never actually climbed it though, I believe," he added as Rachel turned her head to stare at him. "Just caught a glimpse from a railway carriage as he passed on the way to Shropshire. But maybe that's all a poet needs."

Rachel didn't answer. Lorne was looking straight ahead and she found herself examining his profile. It was as craggy as the Welsh mountains, and as implacably strong; yet there was a sensitivity about the eyes and mouth that she hadn't noticed before — hadn't wanted to, perhaps. Her attention was drawn to his hands, resting lightly on the steering wheel. The long fingers also spoke of sensitivity; they looked as if they ought to belong to a musician — a pianist, perhaps, or a violinist. She thought of them on the strings of a Stradivarius, drawing out the sweet, poignant notes that never failed to bring tears to her eyes; and then she thought of them as an instrument of love, touching a woman's face, trailing gently down her neck, seeking out the intimate places with a tenderness that would have her swooning in his arms . . .

Her mind jerked and she turned her face away, conscious of a sudden scorch of heat. What was she doing, letting her thoughts stray this way? Suppose Lorne had noticed, had realised what was going through her mind . . . She stole a glance at him, but to her relief his attention appeared to be entirely occupied by the road ahead. A tiny smile played about his lips, but that could be merely pleasure in the afternoon, in the car he was driving. She hoped devoutly that it was.

"Not far now," he remarked conversationally, and relief swept through her tense body. He hadn't noticed, then. "Garfield Holt lives with his daughter in a rather nice Cotswold manor house, not too big, what they'd call a 'gentleman's country residence', I suppose, but very attractive. I suppose if you're a property magnate you do get first choice of all the best places."

"But he's mostly to do with city property, isn't he?" Rachel queried. "Doesn't he own some tower block in London?"

"Oh, more than one. Yes, he's very much in the millionaire bracket, is Mr Holt. Or Sir Garfield as we'll no doubt be calling him before long. If not Lord Holt." Lorne smiled again. "Strange how we still reward material success with titles, while the real landed gentry are having to sell up their stately homes, or open them to the public just to make ends meet."

Rachel wondered if there might be a touch of bitterness in those words. Lorne's family went back to the Normans, she knew, and although he was clearly not in any financial need, she had heard that the family had gone through a very perilous time only two or three decades earlier. It had been touch and go whether Quentin's could carry on, Mike had told her, in spite of their reputation, for the family had no money apart from what the business made. Perhaps Lorne was jealous of Garfield Holt, who had come up from nothing and was now in line for a knighthood.

"Well, you haven't needed to open your house to the public," she observed coolly. "Only build a car factory in the grounds." She slid her eyes sideways to see how he

111

took that, but apart from a slight tight-
ening of his jawline there was no reaction
and she felt unexpectedly ashamed of her
unwarranted cattiness. But that's the effect
Lorne Quentin has, she told herself resent-
fully. He brings out the worst in me —
makes me the kind of person I don't like.
That's why I don't enjoy being with him.

Before she could pursue this line of
thought, Lorne slowed down and swung
the car in through a pair of tall pillars of
creamy Cotswold stone. Large wrought-
iron gates stood open and the drive curved
ahead between green banks until it came in
sight of a long, low house built of the same
mellow stone, gay now with a profusion of
early roses that scrambled around the door
and windows, and roofed with lichen-
encrusted tiles. Rachel could not repress a
gasp of pleasure as Lorne brought the car
to a halt. She got out and stood gazing at
the slumbering house. As Lorne came
round the car to her side, she turned to
him with parted lips, her eyes shining.

"It's beautiful," she said, and he nodded.

"It is. It's not his only home, of course,
he has a place in London and another in
the Bahamas. As well as various little
pieds-à-terre dotted around here and there.
As a matter of fact, I don't believe he uses

this one a lot — probably won't keep it all that long; these people like to move on and as manor houses go this is a small one."

"I'll believe you." Rachel stood drinking in the peaceful serenity of the scene. How could anyone bear to part with such a house once they owned it? And in such lovely surroundings too — she turned and found herself looking out from the plateau on which the house was built, over a wide panorama of rolling meadows and woods. Here and there she could glimpse the yellowed stone of a cluster of cottages, with an occasional church tower rising, sturdy and four-square, to denote a larger village. But there was nothing bigger; nothing ugly or intrusive. The scene looked, she thought, much as it must have done for centuries, and only the distant sound of a tractor working in the fields served as a reminder that she was still in the twentieth century.

She turned as the front door of the house opened and a maid invited them in. Lorne stood aside and Rachel went through into a panelled hall, the air rich with the scent of wood-polish. She followed the maid through a door and found herself in a pleasant sitting-room, long and low, with windows looking out towards the view she had just been admiring, and a large stone fireplace indicating that the house was as pleasant and comfortable in winter as it was in summer.

"Ah, Lorne." A large man wearing a business suit that looked out of place in this pleasant, chintzy room, came forward and held out his hand. "Glad you could come. And this is your secretary, I take it?" His small eyes swept over Rachel with polite, condescending admiration. His voice was confident and powerful, slightly roughened by traces of a Birmingham accent.

"My Assistant Designer, Miss Grant," Lorne said impassively, and the plump forehead creased as almost-invisible eyebrows lifted. "When I say assistant, I mean of course that Rachel is assistant to my Chief Designer. She will, in fact, be working very closely indeed on the designs for your cars and I wanted her to be in on our discussions from the beginning. You'll find her ideas both sound and progressive."

Wow! Rachel thought, trying to remain as impassive as Lorne. I *must* have impressed him — he wouldn't have said that a month ago! Well, if he was going to support her like that it behoved her to jus-

tify that support. Produce good work —
which she would have done anyway, of
course — but with that extra spark that
only faith and encouragement could draw
from her; which she had expected to have
to get from Mike, but which would be so
much more inspiring coming from
Lorne . . .

"Well." Garfield Holt seemed a little
nonplussed. "Well, if you say so, of course.
I'll have to make it clear, though, Lorne,
this is very much a man's car we want. I'm
not sure . . ." His voice trailed off as his
eyes returned to Rachel, taking in her
slender curves in the pale, clinging silk.
Obviously, she thought in some amusement, he still lived in a world where
women knew their place and kept to it.

Didn't he have any women executives?
she wondered. Were there really still firms
where men held all the top positions?

"I'm sure you'll be very satisfied," Lorne
said smoothly. "And now, if we could perhaps make a start?" He laid his briefcase
on a table and began to open it. Garfield
Holt came to attention with a jerk.

"Oh, yes, yes, of course." Once again, his
small eyes strayed towards Rachel as if he
couldn't quite believe in her existence, and
she returned his look with a gravity she

was beginning to find difficult to maintain. "Yes," he said again, pulling himself together. "Er, let's go through to my study, we can work better there. This way, Miss, er, Grant. Um, yes, this way."

As the property tycoon turned away to lead them out of the room, Rachel glanced at Lorne and bit her lip at his quizzical expression. Much more of this and she'd be suffering a very unbusinesslike fit of the giggles, she thought sternly, and took a deep breath to steady herself. The best thing would be to get down to a serious discussion as soon as possible — take her mind off Garfield's stunned reaction and get that wicked twinkle out of Lorne's eyes . . .

"I thought you'd appreciate Garfield," Lorne murmured later when their host had excused himself for a few minutes. "I know how you like a man who sees women for what they really are . . . All right, all right, I'm sorry," he added hastily as Rachel turned fiercely on him. "I *am* only joking, you know." He grinned reminiscently. "His face when I told him you were my designer! But I think he's getting used to the idea now, Rachel. You've certainly impressed him with some of your ideas."

"Thank goodness," Rachel said feelingly.

"I have an idea you brought me here as a kind of test, Lorne Quentin — just to see how I *could* cope with clients who didn't take me seriously. Am I right?" She looked up at him, eyes green with challenge, and he shrugged deprecatingly.

"Well, perhaps. But not entirely. I'd already committed myself this morning, hadn't I? No, I must admit I was looking forward to your meeting with Garfield Holt. I knew pretty well what his reaction would be but I was intrigued to see yours."

"In other words, you were having your own private little game with us," she accused him, and the mischievous grin lit his rather sombre features once again, making such a difference that she gasped.

"I have to plead guilty, ma'am," he confessed. "You won't be too hard on me, will you?" But before she could answer — and just as well, she thought as her heart jumped a little under Lorne's twinkling gaze — Garfield Holt returned and announced that there was tea ready for them in the sitting-room.

"I think we've done all we can for now," he said, leading them back. "You can be drawing up something along the lines we've been discussing and then we'll have another meeting. Ah, Kelita!" His voice changed, softened with indulgence and Rachel looked past him to see a girl sitting back in one of the low, chintz-covered sofas. "I didn't think you'd be back yet. Had a good day, have you?" He moved towards the girl, beaming down at her, and she gave him a brief smile, her gaze going immediately to Lorne. After a slight hesitation, he went on: "This is Lorne Quentin — Quentin Motors, you know — and this is Miss Grant, his Assistant Designer." A tinge of pride crept into his voice. "My daughter, Kelita."

Rachel watched as the girl's indolent glance moved over her. She showed about as much interest in Rachel as she would have in a shop-window dummy, her clothes coming in for a much sharper examination. There was a noticeable increase in interest when the cool eyes moved back to Lorne, their blueness brightening with a gleam that was very nearly predatory.

"Lorne Quentin?" The girl — she couldn't have been more than eighteen — sat up and lifted her hand for Lorne to take, holding the backs of the fingers towards him as if she were royalty. Lorne held it impassively, and as he let it go a faint pout — had she expected him to *kiss* it, for goodness sake? — touched Kelita's full red lips.

She was a mixture of assured sophistication and youthful naivety, Rachel thought, remembering her own growing-up years when she hadn't even begun to know about the complexities of men and women. Kelita evidently knew a good deal — or thought she did. At any rate, she was well aware of her own attractions and the effect they could have.

No doubt the product of years at the best boarding-school Garfield Holt's money could buy, she was all poise and polish. Slim, with full breasts that were clearly unrestricted by a bra, their budding roundness noticeably outlined by the silky material of a white sundress that would have been an eyecatcher at a cocktail party, demurely high-necked at the front while the back plunged to below the slender waist. Not that Rachel blamed Kelita for wanting to show off such a slim, brown back, nor for letting her soft, pale blonde hair flow down it like a gleaming waterfall. Every girl had the right to make the most of her natural endowments. But she had an idea that Kelita was the kind of girl who used them for one purpose only — as bait to catch any personable male who happened to swim by.

And Lorne was certainly personable. The fact that he must be a good twenty years older than Kelita would only make him all the more interesting; a quarry that any keen young huntress would find an irresistible challenge.

Not, she thought cynically, that Lorne was likely to play very hard to get.

All the same, she hadn't been quite prepared for Lorne's obvious enjoyment of the situation. He must have been well aware of Kelita's almost blatant interest; sophisticated as the young girl was, she wasn't yet experienced enough to conceal it, and she flirted with him openly, opening her Caribbean-blue eyes wide at him, fluttering long dark eyelashes, listening to him with soft lips slightly parted to show pearly white teeth. Every now and then, she would push artlessly at her long swathe of hair, brushing it back from her smooth face with slim fingers that lingered suggestively against her neck.

As a performance, it was almost a caricature, and Rachel could have sworn that Lorne wouldn't be taken in for a second. Yet he was playing up to Kelita for all he was worth, giving her that devastating leprechaun smile, quirking his craggy brows and sending her those glinting, silvery looks that seemed to promise heaven just round the corner. If he wasn't sincere — and how could he be? — it was little short of cruelty. He must know that Kelita, by her very youth, had to be inexperienced, at least with a man of his age. Even if she was asking for it, she needed protection — protection from herself as much as from Lorne or any other ruthless male out for what he could get. She could end up with very burnt fingers indeed if she played with the fire that smouldered in Lorne Quentin.

Rachel glanced at Garfield, but he was watching his daughter with a fond indulgence that told her he was completely besotted, that he saw the flirtatious tricks as nothing more than the endearing ways of a child. As if to endorse her thoughts, he leaned towards Rachel and said in a low voice: "Smashing kid, isn't she, Miss Grant? I know I oughtn't to say so myself, but, well, since her mother died I've had to bring her up on my own, and I flatter myself I haven't made a bad job of it. What do you think?"

Rachel looked again at Kelita. She was handing Lorne a plate of scones, allowing her bare arm to brush against his sleeve as she did so. 'Smashing kid' wasn't exactly the term Rachel would have used to describe her — 'spoiled, precocious brat' would have been nearer the mark, if you could call an eighteen-year-old precocious — but there was still something faintly touching about the younger girl's striving. You really don't have to work so hard at it, Rachel mused as if trying to send her thoughts to Kelita. You're quite attractive enough to just sit back and let it happen. She realised that Garfield was waiting for an answer, and said hastily: "She's very beautiful. Does she take after her mother?"

"You mean she doesn't look a scrap like me." He laughed. "It's all right, Miss Grant, I've never flattered myself I'm any oil-painting. Yes, she gets more like her mother every day. In looks, that is." He paused, his heavy face settling into lines of sadness Rachel hadn't noticed before. "My Jeanie was a real beauty, Miss Grant, a real beauty. I never knew what she saw in me, but we were very happy together. She died when Kelita was seven years old, and since then —" he spread his broad, fleshy hands "— well, life's never been quite the same, if you take my meaning. Jeanie was all the world to me and I've never really felt like marrying again. Well, I had my work, I could give all the time I liked to that and I've never been afraid of hard work. But I don't know quite what I would have done if I hadn't had my little girl to worry about. She became my world instead. Not that I expect to keep her to myself much longer." His eyes strayed again to the tossing blonde hair, the laughing, flirtatious eyes. "I can see she's growing up fast. The young men aren't going to leave her alone much longer." He had been speaking almost abstractedly, but now he seemed to recollect himself and he gave Rachel a quick, embarrassed smile. "Well, I don't know why I'm bothering you with all this, Miss Grant, I'm sure. I flatter myself I keep my worries to myself normally." He laughed again, still embarrassed. "You must have a sympathetic face."

Rachel spoke quickly, reaching out to lay her hand on his arm. She had felt herself warm to the businessman with his gravelly voice and slightly roughened accent, and she wondered if his daughter appreciated the way he felt about her. It was wrong to make snap judgements, she knew, but she'd have taken bets on Kelita's being the kind of spoilt darling who saw her father more as a source of money than a person who needed to be loved. She hoped that she was wrong, that Kelita's brittle, polished exterior hid an affection for her father as deep as his for her. Just at the moment, watching the fluttering, intimate glance Kelita was casting at Lorne, it didn't seem very likely.

But then, she'd have sworn that Kelita's rather obviously-flaunted charms wouldn't have appealed to Lorne, that he would have preferred a more subtle approach, and it looked as if she could be wrong about that, too.

At last they got up to go back to the study, although there was little more to do at this stage and they simply gathered their papers together, watched by Kelita who had accompanied them with her arm hooked through Lorne's as if they were going in to a formal supper.

"You must come again," she said, turning to him with a studied impulsiveness that had her silvery-blonde hair swinging against her bare shoulders. "Mustn't he, Daddy? Come to our cocktail party next week. It's going to be awfully dreary, all Daddy's business friends." She stopped, wrinkling her nose charmingly. "Oh dear, that isn't very enticing, is it! Why should you want to come to a party that's going to be dreary?" She hugged his arm, peeping up into his face. "It won't be dreary if *you* come," she said ingenuously, and Rachel wondered suddenly if all this naivety were simply part of her act. She *couldn't* be quite so wide-eyed and innocent as all that, surely? Not these days.

"You might remember that Mr Quentin is one of my business friends himself," Garfield said, but his tone was of fond indulgence more than reproof, and Rachel realised that the act was probably for his benefit. It suited Kelita at the moment to appear before her father as a child still. Alone with Lorne, she would probably behave quite differently, unless she decided that he liked that approach too, and she would have no scruples at all about reminding her father that she was grown up when that suited her better.

"Oh lord, so he is!" The innocent dismay was very well done — or am I just being catty? Rachel wondered. Kelita smiled up at Lorne in mock apology. "What *must* you be thinking of me? Of course *you're* not dreary." She seemed to notice Rachel then, almost for the first time since they had been introduced. "Is he, Miss Grant?" There was a curious tension in her voice, and Rachel knew that she was trying to find out just what was Lorne's relationship with his Assistant Designer.

Well, you needn't worry about *that*, she thought, and said: "He isn't at all dreary to work for, Miss Holt."

Kelita stared at her with narrowed eyes, then shrugged and gave a tinkling laugh. "Oh, let's forget all these misters and misses, shall we? They're so boring. And we're going to be friends." That was directed at Lorne. "Aren't we?"

"Well, I certainly hope so," Garfield interposed briskly. "But it's business Lorne's here for today, young lady, and I daresay he and Miss Grant want to get on their way now, so we won't keep them any longer." He held out his hand. "I'm very grateful that you could come over this afternoon. It's been a most helpful meeting, most helpful."

"I wish you could stay on for dinner," Kelita mourned, following them to the door. "But I suppose if Rachel's got to get back early . . . You'll have to come in your own car next time, then you won't feel you're dragging him away," she told Rachel with a dazzling smile. "And you *will* come to the cocktail party next week, won't you, Lorne? Do say yes!"

Lorne paused and looked down into the wide, baby-blue eyes. His face was softer than Rachel had ever seen it, his expression an odd blend of amusement and tenderness. It gave her a strange pang, and she bit her lip and turned away.

"I'll let you know," Lorne said, and then he turned and shook Garfield's hand again. "I'll be in touch, Garfield. And if there's anything you need to discuss in the meantime, either Rachel or I will be pleased to come over again. Rachel is going to have personal responsibility for this project, so she'll be up to date with it all the way."

"Goodness, how clever!" Kelita said with her tinkling laugh. "Imagine being able to design cars. I wouldn't know where to start — it's all I can do to decide on the colour! Do you actually *enjoy* doing it, Rachel? I mean, it's a man's job really, isn't it?"

"Some people seem to think so," Rachel answered lightly, "but I don't happen to be one of them. And neither, fortunately, does Lorne. Yes, I enjoy it very much — I wouldn't be much good at it if I didn't." She turned to Garfield. "Thank you for the tea. I'll be seeing you again."

But not at the cocktail party, she thought

as they drove away at last, leaving the mellow stones of the house glowing in the early evening sunshine. Roses scattered tiny spots of colour over the old walls, and flowering shrubs and trees seemed to enclose a world that had little to do with the rat-race outside. She sighed a little at the illusion, for Garfield's study had been equipped with a complex of computer terminals and fax machines that had spewed out information all the time she and Lorne had been there. And his private world, the one shared with Kelita, was as full of tensions and undercurrents as anything outside, even if they weren't yet aware of them. It couldn't be long, surely, before Garfield realised that his daughter was intent on turning into a *femme fatale*, light-years away from the simple child he believed her to be. Or maybe he would never realise it; maybe the scales would always be firmly in place over his eyes.

She remembered that tender look in Lorne's eyes as he'd looked down at the beguiling young face and wondered if that went for him too. Was it only women who could recognise the artifice of a girl like Kelita? Or — and the thought was like a cold knife in her heart — did Lorne see in Kelita another possibility?

Could he possibly be looking for a wife? And could he see Garfield's daughter, sole heiress to the Holt empire, as a suitable Mrs Lorne Quentin?

Five

There was no reason, Rachel told herself as they drove through the twisting Cotswold lanes, to feel that strange coldness in her heart at the thought of Lorne's marrying Kelita Holt, or anyone else. No reason, either, to suppose that he was looking for a wife at all, let alone that he considered Kelita a possible candidate. Hadn't she already assessed him as a man who preferred the freedom of affairs to the commitment of marriage? All the same, most men, even men like Lorne, did eventually get married, if only to have children to whom they could pass on the family name, business, wealth. Lorne had all of those; it wasn't unreasonable that he should be thinking it was time to have a son or daughter who could take over in two or three decades.

It was that look of tenderness, of something else too, that had put the idea into Rachel's mind. She wondered how she would have felt if the look had been directed at her. But it never would be. In Lorne's eyes, she was an experienced woman, no longer an ingenuous child. Perhaps Kelita, with all her youthful naivety that mixed so oddly with her veneer of sophistication, had found the chink in his armour. Perhaps he needed to feel protective towards his women. In which case Rachel, with her hard-won self-sufficiency, was never likely to appeal to him on any basis other than the purely animal one, which was just what she didn't want.

For a moment, she let her mind play with the idea of Lorne as protector, someone whose arms could enfold a woman with something other than passion, a man who would be a rock to lean on, a great tree to shelter under, a strength that could always be trusted . . . She shook herself, thrusting away the image. She didn't *need* it. Hadn't she spent the past few years proving just that?

She remembered something that Kelita had said, and turned to Lorne. "Did you tell Garfield's daughter that I had to be back early? She seemed a little put out that you couldn't stay on."

He smiled. "It seemed a tactful way to allay her obvious disappointment. I suppose if I'd suggested it she would have asked you to stay as well — but somehow I didn't think you'd want that any more than she did."

He was right, but Rachel felt irritated by his assumption that he knew what she'd want. "I was quite happy, talking to Garfield," she said. "He's an interesting man. Not the money-minded tycoon you'd think at first glance."

"A rough diamond?" Lorne said. "Heart of gold under the bluff exterior, and all that? You could be right. He obviously thinks the world of his daughter."

"Let's hope she never lets him down, then," Rachel said, and Lorne shot her a quick glance.

"You didn't care for the society miss?"

"I don't know enough about her to care or not care. Anyway, she's very young. I'm just thinking of the life she's lived — apple of her father's eye, given everything she could want."

"Everything except a mother," Lorne commented softly.

"Well, yes." Rachel was nonplussed. "But that was a long time ago and Garfield's done his best to make up for that, sending her to expensive boarding-schools, helping her to mix with all kinds of people. As a result, she's grown up completely different from him. He's a self-made man — I don't suppose his parents had a penny to bless themselves with. He's had a hard life and he's made good. Kelita's had everything easy. I'm sure all her friends are from wealthy backgrounds, from families that go back for centuries, families with money, connections —"

"Families like mine, in fact," Lorne said, and there was a hard edge to his voice.

Rachel caught herself up. How could she have been so tactless! She had never given a thought to Lorne's background, but it was plain that he would have far more in common with Kelita, with the circles she moved in, than he would have with Garfield, or with Rachel herself. No wonder he'd got along so well with the girl; he hadn't been playing up to her at all, he'd simply been responding naturally to manners, talk, customs that were familiar to him.

So it wouldn't really be too surprising, after all, if Lorne did see Kelita as a possible future wife.

She was saved from hunting for an answer by their arrival in Broadway, one of the most popular of the Cotswold villages, much visited by American tourists. Several of them were in the ancient inn where Lorne had booked dinner, filling the air

133

with their voices as they described to each other where they had been that day, the delightful villages, the charming churches.

"Have you been to Bourton-on-the-Water yet?" one plump, middle-aged woman was asking a young couple. "It's so *pretty*. All those little bridges across the stream, and the little shops are real neat, you've just got to go there."

"And Snowshill," someone else cut in, "you'd never believe the collections they've got in that old house — thousands and thousands of things, a different collection in every room. And the cute little cottages, all clustered round the village green, why, I just wanted to pick the whole thing up and take it back home with me!"

Lorne caught Rachel's eye and grinned. He seemed to have recovered from his brief sharpness in the car. "Someone did," he murmured to her. "The blacksmith's forge from Snowshill was bought and taken home by an American who wanted something different in souvenirs. And someone else once made an offer for the entire village of Broadway, so I've heard — but I've always suspected that story is apocryphal."

"Well, at least it proves they've got an eye for beauty," Rachel said. "I don't much like the idea of our old buildings leaving the country, but at least it's better than being knocked flat in the name of motorways."

"And you a car designer!" he exclaimed. "Where would we be today without the motorway? It keeps juggernauts out of city centres, anyway."

"Some of them," Rachel allowed, thinking of the smaller towns that still suffered a constant barrage of noise and vibration from huge vehicles that could scarcely negotiate the narrow streets. "I don't know what the answer is. I love designing cars and seeing my designs put into practice, but I don't like traffic *en masse*. Perhaps I'm a hypocrite."

"No more than the rest of us, I guess," Lorne said. "We all want the fruits of progress and civilisation, but none of us are too eager to pay the price." He took a menu from the waiter who had come over to the inglenook, filled with copper pans and trailing ferns, where they were sitting. "What would you like to drink?"

Rachel asked for a glass of kir and studied the menu, finding the array of dishes so tempting that it was difficult to choose. She was beginning to relax, to enjoy being here with Lorne. They discussed the choice, taking their time; finally, Rachel settled for *ceviche,* followed by guard of honour with duchesse potatoes and courgettes. Lorne picked watercress soup, followed by fillet steak *en croute,* then chose a red wine that would go with both meals. The menus handed back to the waiter, he sat back, smiled at Rachel and lifted his glass.

"So," he said, letting his smoky eyes rest on her in a way that she found unaccountably disturbing, "what do we do now? Indulge in small-talk, light conversation, or discuss serious issues of the day?"

"I imagined you'd want to discuss Mr Holt's order," Rachel answered, uncomfortably aware of his thoughtful gaze, but Lorne shook his head.

"Didn't we agree it was a mistake to mix business with pleasure?" he countered. Rachel immediately wanted to reply that as far as she was concerned this was a business occasion — she would never have agreed to come out to dinner with him otherwise. She didn't say so, however; she didn't want those silvery eyes to widen with mockery, even though she would certainly have liked them to stop looking at her in the way they were just at present . . .

"Tell me what you thought of Garfield

Holt," he said suddenly. "As a man, rather than a business associate."

Rachel gave him a cautious look, wondering why it should matter to him what she thought of Garfield. But he was probably just making conversation, and at least it kept his mind off her. Here, away from the factory, she was finding it increasingly difficult to retain her cool detachment. And the memory of that kiss had begun to intrude disturbingly on her thoughts.

"I wasn't sure at first," she said slowly. "He seemed to be the typical self-made man — hard, ruthless, immersed in his business empire. But then his daughter arrived and, well, he changed. Showed a softer side. As you say, he obviously thinks the world of her. He told me himself, she *is* his world. That's why I think he could be very badly hurt if she —"

"If she what? Lets him down? In what way do you think she might do that?"

Rachel shrugged helplessly. "How does any child let its parents down? By just not loving them, I suppose. Taking all they can give and then leaving them with nothing. I think that apart from that, almost anything Kelita did would be all right with Garfield. Just so long as she stays, well, stays his daughter."

"But you don't think she will? You think she'll squeeze everything she can out of him and then take off? You think she's that shallow, that ruthless?"

Rachel glanced at him. There was an edge to his voice that was almost urgent. She looked away, concentrating her gaze on a bowl of roses that stood on a small table near his elbow. Why should it matter so much to him what kind of person Kelita Holt was?

"I don't know. How can I, after only an hour or so in their company? She just strikes me as a very spoilt child, with not much thought for anyone but herself. But she's young, she could grow out of that. It could be just a phase." She watched while Lorne twirled his glass thoughtfully between his fingers. "I don't really think we ought to be gossiping about the Holts like this, anyway," she said stiffly, and to her surprise Lorne gave her his quick, unexpectedly mischievous grin.

"Certainly we shouldn't — but it's rather fun, isn't it!" His eyes danced suddenly and Rachel laughed and relaxed almost in spite of herself. Maybe it didn't matter after all, maybe he wasn't seriously interested in Kelita. "I've often thought I'd like to write a gossip column," he continued.

"You know, find out everyone's wicked secrets and tell the world. I'd never really do such a thing, of course, it's just a fantasy, but a fairly harmless one. It's just that the life is so completely different from mine — spending your days in Fleet Street, going to all the best places to eat just to see what the celebrities are up to." His eyes rested on Rachel's face, as impossible to read as woodsmoke. "What fantasies do you have, Rachel? Tell me."

At once, she was on edge again. "I don't have any fantasies," she said quickly, and he smiled and shook his head.

"Nonsense — everyone has fantasies. Some of them quite amazing." The dark red kir glowed in his glass. "Perhaps you bury yours somewhere deep down, is that it? A mistake, I'm afraid — you should take them out, look at them, enjoy them. Try it sometime."

Rachel began to wish the waiter would come to tell them their table was ready, though she doubted whether simply moving into another room would change the direction of Lorne's thoughts. She didn't know quite what to make of him tonight. He seemed to have shed the cool remoteness he normally displayed, becoming a different person — probing, inquisitive, disconcerting. She had the uncomfortable feeling that she'd had before, that those gleaming eyes could look right through into her mind and see the confused tangle of thoughts and emotions that his words were stirring into life. And not just his words — his glance, his touch as he passed her the little bowl of olives, even the way he was sitting, body turned towards her yet totally relaxed, as if he had full command of both himself and her.

That was what she found most disturbing, the feeling that she was no longer in complete control, that somewhere along the line she had become little more than a puppet in Lorne's hands, that he had only to flick a string and she would move to his bidding.

But that was ridiculous! It must be the effect of drinking kir on an empty stomach — it seemed a long time since that scone she'd eaten at Garfield's house, and she had had only the lightest of snack lunches in her hurry to be ready when Lorne called. The sooner she had something to eat, the sooner she would feel normal again. This dizzy feeling of being not quite in control, this turmoil of uncertainty, neither had anything to do with Lorne really. They would disappear once she had had some food.

"Do you know what I think?" Lorne was saying now in that soft, caressing voice that did such tingling things to her nerve-ends. "I think that all your feelings are so tightly bottled-up inside you that you hardly know what's there. Love, hate, bitterness, joy — we've all had a fair measure of them by the time we've been adult for a few years. It doesn't do any good to suppress them, did you know that? It can even do quite a lot of harm."

Fear stirred, like a coiled snake, somewhere deep inside Rachel. How could Lorne Quentin know so much about her? He was her employer, nothing more, an austere man who was interested only in his cars. But there was another side to him too, she reminded herself — a fiery, even violently passionate nature lurked beneath that cool surface. A nature that something in her couldn't help responding to, even though she feared her own response. Yet his voice didn't sound at all dangerous — it was soft, velvety, understanding . . . Confused and scared, she took refuge in the only emotion she felt safe with — anger.

"And is being a psychiatrist another of your fantasies?" she enquired icily. "Probing into other people's minds, drawing out all the things that are best forgotten, living their lives at second-hand? Maybe there's some deep, hidden reason for that too — like, you're afraid of life yourself, afraid to commit yourself deeply to any other person, afraid to do anything more than skate over the surface. As it happens, I think you know very little about me. And now perhaps we could talk about something else. The waiter's coming — our table must be ready."

Lorne inclined his head as if in acquiescence, but Rachel found little comfort in his apparent submissiveness. There was still a gleam in his eye she didn't trust, and a tiny quirk to his lips that told her he wasn't in the least abashed. But then, she thought ruefully as they followed the waiter through to a panelled dining-room glowing with polished copper and vivid flowers, Lorne wasn't the kind of man who *would* be easily discomfited. He was far too sure of himself.

His next words confirmed that view, though at the same time they managed to make her eyes prickle with the realisation that Lorne was, besides being uncomfortably perceptive, much more sensitive than she had supposed. "You know," he said, tilting his head disarmingly to one side, "you're quite right. I do know very little

142

about you. Tell me some more." He paused for no more than a second, then added quietly: "Not the things that are best forgotten. I've no doubt that there are some — we all have a few — and I still hold to the view that they're better brought out into the open. But maybe you'll feel like telling me those another time."

Rachel stared at him. Once again, he had turned her emotions upside down. She'd been ready to feel angry with him, indignant at his intrusion and assumptions; now, for one mad moment, she felt she could tell him anything and he would understand. A crazy longing to do just that shook her. To sit close beside him, held in those strong, warm arms, pour out all the disappointment and grief that had made her what she was now, know that with him she was safe for ever. She wrenched her thoughts away so roughly that she winced. What in God's name was this man doing to her?

"You know all that's necessary, surely," she said woodenly, but he shook his head.

"All that's necessary to recognise you as my Assistant Designer, yes. But there must be much more to know — and I've already told you, I don't mean to pry into your private affairs. Just the ordinary, everyday things. Your family, for instance — you've told me a bit about them, about your brothers and your parents. Do you still see them? Are you as close as when you were growing up? What things have happened to you since you left home — not the career things, just the little, personal things." His smile crinkled at her. "I don't want to know how many lovers you've had, either, not that you'd dream of telling me!"

Rachel's face burned as she gazed speechlessly back at him, and he added, almost as if he had just made a discovery: "I find I'm increasingly curious to know just what kind of person you are, Rachel. You're an enigma, did you realise that?"

"*I'm* an enigma?" she burst out, then bit her lip. It would never do for Lorne to get the idea that she might be just as interested in him — she wasn't, was she? Not really, but the gleam of amusement in his eyes told her he hadn't missed any of the implications of that little exclamation. "Oh, I don't think so," she went on, quickly recovering herself. "There's nothing mysterious about me. It's just that you've never taken any interest."

"So I'm taking an interest now. Tell me."

Rachel cast about wildly for something to talk about, something that would get her through the rest of this evening without giving way to his probing — for probing it was, whatever he might say. "Well, I told you I grew up on Exmoor," she began hesitantly, wondering if Lorne would accept this or whether he would bring her relentlessly back to more intimate issues. But he nodded encouragingly and she went on, telling him about her childhood in the big house so close to the moors where she and her brothers had spent their free time walking, riding, exploring the wild countryside; acting out 'adventures' — *Lorna Doone* had been a favourite game for one whole summer, she remembered — and making camps. They had once killed and cooked a rabbit, she recalled, coping with the grisly business of preparation and roasting it over a wood fire; none of them had had a lot of appetite for the meat and she had found it difficult to face rabbit stew for quite a while after that! And they had even slept out under the stars during the summer holidays, developing a self-reliant independence that had prepared them well for adult life. Without it, Rachel wasn't at all sure that she would have been able to fight for her career as, in the early stages, she'd had to do.

The thought jerked her out of her reminiscences, into the present, and she stopped talking abruptly, feeling her face colour. What on earth must Lorne be thinking of her now, rambling on about her childhood as if it had been something extraordinary? She forgot that she had seized on the subject as an excuse to keep off anything more revealing, and said ruefully: "I'm sorry. I seem to have told you my entire life-history. You must be bored rigid."

"Not in the least." Lorne eyed her thoughtfully. He didn't tell her that her green eyes were sparkling with happy memories, her oval face alive with animation, all her reserve shed as she relived those carefree days. "I've been fascinated." She gave him a quick glance, but there wasn't a trace of mockery in either his face or his voice. "You've been very lucky."

"Yes, I have," Rachel agreed soberly. She had seen enough ill-assorted families since leaving home to realise just how fortunate she had been, to understand the importance of a secure childhood in preparing the way for a balanced adult life. Helping herself to a roast potato, she enquired, "What sort of childhood did you have?"

"Not quite as idyllic as yours, I'm afraid," he answered shortly. "Only child, rather solitary, spent most of my time at boarding-school or staying with other boys. Nothing very interesting at all." Absently, he sliced a piece of steak, then returned his gaze to Rachel's face. "And since you left school, what then? College, I know. That must have meant leaving home. Did you miss your family very much, or did you find other consolation? I can't imagine a girl like you being without boyfriends."

Here it came, Rachel thought. The real reason behind all this probing. The question Lorne had been leading up to all this time, in spite of his disclaimers; the question of her love-life, as her mother would have delicately phrased it. Or, as she had no doubt Lorne would more bluntly have said, her sex-life. Well, maybe it wasn't so surprising that he should be interested. A girl didn't reach the age of twenty-eight without having had *some* kind of relationship.

It just happened that she didn't have the slightest intention of telling him about it. That moment of madness, when she'd wanted to pour out everything into those too-willing ears had passed and she'd guard against it ever coming back.

"I've had boyfriends, yes," she said

lightly. "Not a lot, as it happens. I was really more interested in my work."

"Really?" His eyebrows quirked upwards. "*Always?* Haven't you ever had anyone special? Anything serious?"

Rachel shrugged. "Depends what you call serious. I've never been engaged, if that's what you mean." And she hadn't, not in the old-fashioned sense. Not with a ring on her finger, a party, wedding plans . . . She sighed, unable to prevent a faint twist of pain from touching her face, and turned her head quickly as she caught Lorne's glance sharpening.

But perhaps he hadn't noticed anything after all. He didn't say anything for a moment or two; then, to her relief, he turned his attention back to his steak.

"We're not all the marrying kind," he said casually, and Rachel had a sharp reminder of her earlier summing-up of his own inclinations — that he was a man who would have affairs rather than a permanent commitment. And wasn't this what all this was leading up to? His encouragement of her childhood memories, his artless questions about her life since leaving home, and then this final remark — wasn't it all a prelude to the pass he would no doubt make when he took her home? He already knew that there was a vibrant chemistry between them, that her response to his kisses was immediate and satisfying. So naturally he'd try again.

It was probably the line he took with all attractive women, Rachel thought wearily. Or maybe he was more subtle than that — sensitive enough to gauge exactly which approach would work best with each woman he desired. She remembered his behaviour with Kelita, the way he'd responded in kind to the young girl's open flirting. A less sensitive man might have treated Rachel in the same way, taking the line that all women were the same and enjoyed the same advances. But Lorne had acknowledged the fact that Rachel was ten years older than Kelita and probably considerably more experienced. He had seen that she would respond to a more serious approach. And, damn him, taking into account the fact that she was already far too strongly attracted to him, he was right.

What he didn't know was that Rachel's experience was of the kind that armed her against any further mistakes; the kind that, the more strongly she was attracted, the more likely she was to withdraw into herself, erect all her barricades, become a tightly self-contained fortress. Her experience had been too bitter and painful to risk any repetition, however strong the temptation.

From then on, to Rachel's relief, Lorne turned his attention to less personal matters. For the rest of the meal they discussed a variety of different subjects, surprising Rachel with the breadth of Lorne's interests and the depth of his knowledge. Together, they discovered a mutual love of orchestral music, especially the Russian composers, and a liking for classical guitar and certain kinds of jazz. Neither of them liked pop music, but Lorne declared that he was 'into heavy metal' and Rachel confessed to a weakness for fifties-style ballads. They both enjoyed reading too, Rachel being more at home with Jane Austen and Dickens while Lorne surprised her with his knowledge of Shakespeare and the Lake poets; they both read crime novels avidly, but Rachel didn't tell Lorne that she still occasionally lost herself in one of her childhood school stories.

From books and poetry they ranged to the theatre and were astonished to find that they must have attended a performance of *The Mousetrap* on the same night, a year earlier. When they came to films and Rachel admitted that she must be one of the last people in Britain who had never seen *The Sound of Music*, Lorne shook his head vigorously, eyes dancing.

"Wrong — there are two of us!" he told her, laughter in his voice. "But why not? Don't tell me there's no romance in your soul — not if you can still weep over Tiny Tim!"

Rachel shook her head, smiling, and wondered briefly that she could feel so relaxed when only an hour ago she'd been like a tightly-coiled spring. "As much as in anyone else's," she answered. "I don't really know why not — perhaps because it's been hyped so much. And I had a feeling it might be just too sugary, but I could be wrong about that."

"I know what you mean, I guess I reacted in the same way. Well, there's only one way to find out whether we're right or not — we'll have to see it together. At least we'll both be safe from misty-eyed sentimentality."

Rachel smiled, taking his suggestion as the joke it must have been. But she was conscious of a tiny moment of hurt. Had she given him the impression she was so hard-boiled? The moment was over almost before she recognised it, and Lorne was signing the credit card slip for the bill. In the hiatus, Rachel felt her easy mood evaporate, leaving a chilly apprehension. Here, in this comfortable inn with other people around them it had been easy to relax. But what now? There was still the drive home to be faced, still that moment when they would arrive at her cottage in its quiet lane. Would Lorne be content to leave her with a brief good-night, or would he be expecting something more?

It wasn't a new situation, and Rachel had never had any difficulty in dealing with it before. But maybe that was because she'd never had a date with a man who affected her in quite the way Lorne did; maybe she'd subconsciously avoided the risk. Just as she would have done now, only this dinner with Lorne had come upon her unexpectedly, giving her no chance to refuse. And she certainly *would* have refused, she thought. No way would she have come out with Lorne on a conventional date. He was too virile, too dominating, too downright attractive.

And there was another reason. This time, Rachel had something to fear that was inside herself. A deep, yearning ache that was new to her; a sensation she wasn't at all sure she could control.

She followed Lorne to the car as if she

were in a dream, saying nothing as she got in, and settled herself in the passenger seat. Lorne sat beside her, equally silent. It was as if he were aware that she had withdrawn into her own private world and respected it; as if he had decided not to try to draw her out any further. Or was it because he too was deep in thought, absorbed by — what? Regret that it wasn't Kelita, young and willing, his for the taking, beside him? Or maybe he was just bored, thankful that the evening would soon be over.

Rachel looked out at the moon-bathed landscape. There was little traffic on the quiet roads. Hills rose and fell like shadows, and the sky was the clear, dusky blue of summer nights, lit by a rising moon that dimmed the few stars pricking through the darkness. They passed a few country pubs, bright light and laughter spilling from open doors and windows onto grassy gardens or narrow streets. Once, on a stretch of empty road, the headlamps picked up two glowing green points, and as they came nearer they saw a fox turn away and disappear into a hedge.

It was all a million miles and a thousand light-years away from what had happened to Rachel four years ago, when she was in her first real job and taking those first tentative steps up the ladder that had become her reason for living. And Lorne was as different from Graham as a man could be.

So why did she keep thinking of those days? Was it just because Lorne had put her in the mood for remembering — even those 'things best forgotten'? Why, when she had thought herself completely recovered from the pain, did it nag at her again, like the ache of a drawn tooth?

Rachel had been just twenty-three when she first met Graham Beech. She had only recently completed her sandwich course at college, sponsored by a car manufacturer. It had been hard work, nearly five years in all, her college terms interspersed with periods in the factory, going through all the processes of car design and manufacture. But she'd completed it at last, together with the year's contracted work which was part of the deal, and now she was free to move if she wished.

She hadn't wanted to move, however. The firm had been good to her, even taking her on at all as a sandwich student had been a boost they might have preferred not to give a girl, and she felt a loyalty towards them. She knew, too, that she still had plenty to learn. And on top of that, there was Graham.

Graham had joined the firm's design team at just about the time Rachel completed her course. He was four years her senior, confident and assured. Later on, she'd recognised his assurance as brashness, but she'd admired and envied it then. Tall, with bright brown hair and merry eyes, he'd captivated her from that first morning, and she'd found herself laughing helplessly at his jokes, agreeing to have lunch with him, and then dinner, and then lunch next day; and, before the week was out, falling hopelessly in love with him.

She'd often reflected since that she might not have fallen quite so hard or so quickly if she'd had any real experience of love before. But, in an odd sort of way, growing up with three brothers had been a handicap rather than a help in her adult relationships with men. As a child, she'd quickly learned that her more feminine qualities should be concealed if she wanted to keep up with her brothers. Dolls and tea-parties were out, meccano, camping and cricket were all-important. It hadn't worried Rachel, who was quite happy to become the complete tomboy and could climb higher trees, swim wider rivers and run faster races than any girl and quite a few boys she knew. But it hadn't stood her in good stead when she reached adolescence and found herself trying to cope with a disturbing new set of emotions in herself, and entirely different reactions in boys.

For quite a while, she'd floundered. The boys she was interested in now didn't seem to appreciate her ability to climb, swim, run — it seemed almost as if they were put off by it. Their response to her left her feeling confused and slightly scared. And the girls she knew seemed to belong to some secret society with rules she didn't understand, giggling over jokes she only vaguely comprehended. They knew all about make-up and clothes, things Rachel had previously dismissed with scorn and now found mystifying and frustrating.

It didn't help when she reached college and found herself the only girl taking engineering, with little opportunity to mix with girls on other courses. And as a defence against the rather unnerving reactions of the rest of the group she became even more 'one of the boys', dressing in jeans and baggy sweaters that hid her curving figure, scrubbing her face clean of the make-up she'd never properly learned to use, dragging her rich auburn hair back from her face and fastening it with nothing more glamorous than an elastic band.

She might have gone on like this for a long time, lonely and bewildered, convinced that no man would ever find her attractive, if it had not been for Annette.

Annette was in the year below her, a small, lively, prettily blonde girl who was clearly delighted with her own femininity and considered that to be the only girl on a course was the biggest piece of luck in her life. The two girls found themselves thrown together quite a lot, and Rachel was at first startled, then intrigued by Annette's air of unassumed coquetry and her undoubted popularity with the male students. They gathered round her like bees round a hive, and Annette made no secret of her enjoyment of their attentions; yet she never played one against another, never cheated them, and seemed able to keep them all in love with her, vying for her favours without creating jealousy.

It wasn't long before she took Rachel severely in hand.

"You're crazy not to make more of yourself," she said bluntly one day. "That marvellous hair, and your *figure*. You could knock 'em cold if you'd only be yourself —

what you're meant to be. Don't you see that?"

"But what *am* I meant to be?" Rachel asked, bemused.

"Well, a *woman*, of course — what else?" Annette flung up her hands and turned her eyes to the ceiling. "Look, I believe in having fun in this world, or what's the point of it all? And I can't sit back and see you letting life pass you by. We'll start with your hair and make-up, then we'll go shopping for some decent clothes. And then I'll teach you a few tricks of the trade."

Rachel had watched her own transformation with a kind of wonder. And from then on, her life had improved. Within a month, she had her first date; within six months, a string of boyfriends almost as long as Annette's.

None of them had been serious, though — she wasn't ready for that. Just have fun, Annette had advised her, and that was what she did. It was enough, until she met Graham. Only then did she begin to want more, and she was still too inexperienced to cope with the stronger urges of her newly-wakened body.

"Rachel," Graham said when he brought her back to her bedsitter after an evening out that had dazzled her. "Rachel, you must know how I feel about you. You're not going to make me leave, are you? Not now, when everything's so marvellous, when we've just found each other . . ." His lips were moving across her face, touching her cheeks, her eyes, the lobes of her ears, returning finally to her mouth which she gave him with a shy eagerness. "Let me love you, Rachel," he breathed, letting one hand slip down to her breast. "Let me show you just how I feel . . ."

After that first night, it seemed stupid to tell Graham he couldn't stay again. And before very long, it had seemed inevitable that they should move into his more spacious flat and live together.

"It's the usual thing these days," he told her when they discussed this move. "Everyone does it. Of course I want to marry you, darling, but we don't want to rush into it, do we? We want to start properly. So in the meantime, where's the sense in being apart? Let's enjoy ourselves first!"

It had only struck Rachel later that Graham spoke of marriage rather as if it marked the end of enjoyment. But in those early days she was still bemused, still fascinated. It was some time before her vision cleared and she saw Graham for what he really was.

In the meantime, she'd been happy. Or so she had told herself, for there were moments when she found herself wondering, with a kind of dismay, just what she was doing and why. Moments when Graham was asleep and she was staring into the darkness, dimly aware that the early promise of excitement induced by his first caresses had never been quite fulfilled. "It's often a bit awkward at first, especially when one of the partners isn't experienced," Graham had told her kindly, making her feel guiltily that it must be her fault. "It'll get better all the time, you'll see." And it had certainly seemed to be satisfying for him — invariably he fell asleep within moments. So why did she continue to lie awake?

There'd been other moments too — like when she'd taken him to Exmoor to meet her family and found them somehow less enthusiastic than she had expected. Nobody had *said* anything, but her parents had welcomed Graham with a politeness that had in itself been disconcerting, and her eldest brother, the only one home at the time, had spent almost all his time out of the house.

"Don't you like Graham?" Rachel asked her mother on the Sunday afternoon, not long before they departed.

"I don't know whether I like him or not. He seems a very nice young man, polite, keen to please. I just, well, you won't like my saying this, Rachel, but I'm just sorry you didn't wait to be married."

"Oh, for heaven's sake, Mum!" Rachel said, more crossly than she needed to. "That's old-fashioned. Everyone lives together these days."

"Yes," her mother answered quietly, "I know." And she had refused to say any more.

Rachel had gone back with Graham feeling chilled. It had been a bad start and she felt that their bright love had been somehow tarnished. Graham's reassurances didn't help; she'd always trusted her parents' judgement, and to hear him calling them 'old-fashioned squares' made her want to come to their defence. She was torn in two directions.

But all her worries disappeared when she and Graham worked together, and soon they were spending all their time on a joint project, new designs that were both practical and innovative. Rachel was the one with ideas, Graham the one who could work out the practicalities. When it was time to present their ideas to the chief designer, she saw it as a chance to prove her faith in Graham and allowed him to take the major part in the discussions. Her own part in the project was glossed over almost without her realising it. The discussions took place without her presence, and more and more of them seemed to mean late evenings 'in conference' or meeting the managing director at dinner. Rachel found herself more and more alone.

"Haven't you mentioned me at all?" she asked one night when Graham came back particularly late. "Didn't you tell them we did these designs together?"

Graham looked at her. His face was redder than usual, his bright eyes almost feverish. Rachel felt a stab of fear.

"Something's happened. What is it?"

Graham turned away. They were in the bedroom, Rachel sitting up with the blankets making a hillock over her knees, her face clean of make-up, unaware of just how young and vulnerable she looked.

"Don't start nagging, for God's sake," Graham said thickly. "Can't you see I'm tired?"

Shock silenced Rachel for a moment, then she said in a whisper: "You've got to tell me, Graham. What is it? Please."

For a moment, he said nothing, then he

shrugged and turned back, and Rachel knew as she looked into his shifting eyes that this was the end.

"All right, then," he said heavily. "You might as well know straightaway. I was going to wait for the right moment, but —"

"Tell me!"

"I've been seeing Sue Menton," Graham said baldly. "I . . . well, we've fallen in love. We're going to be married."

The words hung on the air, repeating themselves over and over again, hammering like coffin-nails into Rachel's stunned brain. *Sue Menton . . . fallen in love . . . going to get married . . .* She wanted to clutch at her head, to scream at them to go away. But they wouldn't. They were there for ever, burning into her mind like brands that could never be healed.

"Sue Menton?" she said at last in a dry whisper that was no stronger than the rustle of a dead leaf. "The — the managing director's daughter? You're going to *marry* her?" A tiny flare of anger flickered into blessed life. "You're not going to live with her first?"

"With Sue?" The question seemed to take Graham by surprise. "I can just see her father's reaction to that!"

"No, he wouldn't like it, would he?" Rachel was clutching at her anger, grasping it like a lifeline, knowing it was the only thing that could save her from complete humiliation. "My parents didn't like it much, either, or didn't you notice? But that didn't matter, did it?"

"That was completely different," Graham began, but Rachel cut in sharply. A part of her watched in fascination. She'd had a furious temper as a child, a temper which she'd had to learn to control. It had often started just like this, with a slow burning inside that had exploded with a bang that shook everything around her.

"Different? How was it different? Because my father's only a country doctor and miles away, while Sue Menton's is the managing director? Because marrying me would have done nothing for you, once you'd bled me of all my ideas, while marrying Sue will get you to the top the short way?" She stared at Graham, seeing the deep colour of his face, the way his eyes bulged, and had a sudden vision of him in ten years' time, paunchy and red-nosed. How could she ever have thought him attractive? He was contemptible! "You're nothing but a mean little money-grabber, a man who uses people to get him up the ladder and then kicks them away. You've used me and my designs — because you never did admit that they were mostly mine, did you — and now you'll use Sue." Rachel's green eyes raked him with a flashing scorn that had him turning away. "I'd lay any odds you don't love her, any more than you loved me. You've just exerted your charm over her. It isn't Sue Menton's husband you want to be — it's Robert Menton's son-in-law. Well, good luck to you — and good luck to them, for they're certainly going to need it."

Graham came over to her. There was a look of pleading on his face as he reached out his hands. "Rachel, don't take it like that. It's nothing like what you think. I'm truly sorry. I *did* think I loved you, I swear it, but when Sue and I . . . well, it's different, that's all I can say. After all, no one can help falling in love, can they? Even you —"

"Get out," Rachel said, still keeping a tight hold on her temper. It was like a volcano, seething very close to the surface. She clenched her hands.

Graham put out his hands and laid them on her bare arm. "Rachel. Please —"

The volcano erupted. With a cry of rage that seemed to come from someone else,

Rachel found herself lifting her whole body from the bed as she struck out at him. There was a sharp crack as her hand met Graham's cheek with all the force she could muster, and he staggered back with a cry of pain and astonishment. Rachel didn't give him time to recover. With her other hand, she threw her pillow at him, following it in quick succession with the alarm clock, her book — a good, heavy one, she noted with relish — and finally Graham's pyjamas. The pillow caught him full in the face and the clock hit him on the shoulder. The book hit the pillow as he clawed it away, and the pyjamas draped themselves over his head. He looked so ridiculous that Rachel began to laugh.

"You little virago!" Graham exclaimed, shaking his head like a wounded animal. "I'm not having this. This is my bedroom, Rachel, and my flat, and —"

Rachel's laughter stopped abruptly and her eyes glinted threats at him. "Get out," she said again, her tone dangerous. "I don't care if it is your bedroom, and I warn you I can throw quite heavy things if I have to. I'll go tomorrow — I'll be only too pleased — but for tonight I'm staying right where I am." She met his blustering stare with an icy calmness that was only a thin veneer over the fury still simmering beneath. "Just get out. Now." Without taking her eyes from his, she reached out and unplugged the table lamp.

Graham hesitated; then he stooped and picked up the pyjamas and the pillow.

"All right," he said with an attempt at dignity. "Since you don't seem to be able to discuss this reasonably, I'll leave you. I daresay I can manage to sleep on the couch for tonight. It wouldn't be right to share a bed with you, anyway — not now that I'm engaged to Sue. We'll talk about it tomorrow, when you're in a more reasonable frame of mind."

"And when you're in a less pompous one," Rachel said, and watched him go.

There had been no discussion, of course. There really wasn't anything to talk about. Rachel had packed her things and left the next morning. She had gone into the office only to give in her notice and take the leave that was owing to her — enough to ensure that she needn't come in again. She had refused to allow herself to cry. That could wait until she had got right away, somewhere where she could breathe clean air and begin to think straight, to be herself again, her own person. She felt now as if she'd been possessed, gone temporarily crazy, and she wouldn't let herself cry until she was back to normal.

And by that time, she hadn't wanted to.

Memories came and went like the shadowy hills as Rachel sat beside Lorne in the car. Some were bright and vivid, others faded. In the years between, she had seen Graham for the opportunist he was, and had accepted her own vulnerability. And she had grown a shell around herself as a protection.

Until now, the danger had been slight. Rachel hadn't cut herself off from men; she'd had dates, friendships, but there had always been a very definite line drawn and none of her relationships had progressed further than a casual good-night kiss. So far it had worked; some men had faded from the scene, others had stayed as friends. Nobody but Rachel knew the gnawing loneliness that sometimes attacked her at night. Not for Graham — it was a deep, unassuaged yearning for someone else, someone she'd never met but felt must exist somewhere, someone who could be her other half, who could make her feel complete.

It was a yearning that made her extra vulnerable at times. She could so easily be taken in again, and she couldn't risk that. So when she was more strongly attracted than usual, she found herself withdrawing more sharply.

With Lorne, she felt more vulnerable than ever before.

Not that Lorne would ever cheat her in the way that Graham had. He wouldn't steal her ideas under a pretence of loving her. In all his dealings, Lorne would be honest.

In love, too. An affair with Lorne would be just that — no false promises of marriage. An honest relationship, to be enjoyed by both partners with no strings attached; ended honestly when it had run its course.

And that was just the trouble. Because Rachel knew that an affair with Lorne would involve her too deeply to want it to end. She wasn't the type for casual relationships, experience had taught her that. If she couldn't have a permanent commitment — marriage — she'd rather not have anything.

And marriage with Lorne . . . she shivered suddenly. It wasn't even to be considered.

They were coming to the village where Rachel lived now, driving through the quiet street, turning into the lane that led to her cottage. The moon hung clear and bright over the orchard. Lorne stopped the car outside her gate and Rachel braced herself.

Here it comes, she thought in sudden panic, and I still don't know what to do.

Lorne turned to her. He reached out and with one finger under her chin turned her face towards him. His eyes gleamed like silver in the moonlight, and his fingertip was like a flame against her skin.

"We're here," he said quietly, and she nodded. "What's the matter, Rachel? You're as tight as a spring."

"Nothing." Her voice was dry, husky. "Nothing at all. I'm just a little . . . tired. Thank you for the dinner, Lorne, it was lovely. And I hope everything goes well with Garfield's order."

"I'm sure it will." He watched her thoughtfully, then suddenly reached across, trapping her in his arms. Rachel stiffened and closed her eyes — if he kissed her, she wouldn't be able to resist, she knew it — but Lorne was merely opening the door. He drew back, still watching her, then turned away and got out of the car on his own side.

Feeling weak at the knees, Rachel scrambled out as he came around to open the door properly, and stood facing him in the moonlight. Was he expecting her to ask him in for coffee? She opened her mouth, but no sound came. And as she tried again, Lorne bent towards her and laid his lips on hers.

The kiss was brief and sweet. There was no passion in it; no thrusting tongue, no demands. His lips were cool and tender against her own; yet their touch roused in Rachel a desire more powerful, more urgent than any she had known before, and from the quick intake of Lorne's breath she knew that he had felt it too.

For a long moment, they stared at each other. Lorne's eyes, lit by the glow of the moon, were shimmering pools of mystery, fathomless with emotions Rachel could barely guess at. Her own eyes were wide with uncertainty as she gazed up at him, quivering under his touch, vibrantly aware that it needed only one word from him, one tiny movement, to break down all her fragile defences. In that moment, she was conscious of only two emotions: an aching, yearning desire and a fear that was as much fear of herself as of him. The two sensations were in perfect balance; so that all she could do was stand there, accepting whatever was to come as inevitable.

A change came over Lorne's face as she waited. It was something Rachel couldn't define; a gravity that hadn't been there before, an intent searching of her own expression, a hesitation. Then his lips tightened briefly and he gave her a gentle shake.

"Time you went in," he said quietly. "I'll just wait and see you safely in the front door."

"Oh — yes." Rachel didn't want him to go now, she *wanted* to ask him in for coffee, for any excuse that would hold him with her. Suddenly, unexpectedly, she didn't want the evening to end, didn't want to part from him. But it was as if she had forgotten how to say the words, as if something inside was preventing them. She gave him a smile that felt faint and watery, then turned away quickly, afraid that even now there might be mockery in the lean, dark face. Then she turned and went up the short garden path to her front door, unlocked it and with a final, quick wave, slipped inside.

As if in a dream, she went upstairs, washed and slid into bed. For a moment she wondered if she would sleep at all that night. But it was as if her brain had gone on strike, as if her mind were too stunned to think. And maybe that was the best thing. Because thinking wasn't going to do any good. Not unless she knew what thoughts might be going through Lorne's head. Without them, her own were only half complete.

There was something important there, some germ of knowledge that ought to be clear, ought to make everything else clear. But before Rachel could grasp at it, it had slipped away. She closed her eyes and slept.

Six

Rachel went into her office slowly next morning, conscious of her confused feelings and not sure whether she wanted to see Lorne or avoid him. All the same, her reaction was one of relief when Julie came in with some papers and told her that he'd been called away suddenly to a customer in the north. Relief, followed almost at once by a pang of disappointment.

It was probably just as well he wasn't here, she told herself wryly as she settled down to work. She was potentially on the verge of becoming quite involved with Lorne Quentin, and it just wouldn't do. Really? asked a sardonic little voice inside her. Wasn't she mature enough yet, at twenty-eight years old, to cope with what a man like Lorne Quentin could offer? That business with Graham, it was years ago. Hadn't she grown up at all during those years? Grown up enough to have an affair if she wanted one, to enjoy it as Lorne would enjoy it, to end it when it needed ending and go on without a qualm?

That was the *mature* way to handle it, no doubt. But Rachel wasn't at all sure that she was the kind of woman to do it that way. Maybe it wasn't so much a question of maturity after all; maybe it was something else.

Lorne was away for several days. His journey north was combined with visits to some of their suppliers, and then he had several meetings to attend; the family had acquired other interests besides the motor factory, and these needed attention. Rachel used the respite to try to banish him from her thoughts. She was almost successful, but there were still far too many moments when she found herself, chin on hand, gazing dreamily out of the window and thinking of the evening they'd spent together, the butterfly kiss he'd given her as they parted. But as soon as she realised what was happening, she sat up abruptly and turned her mind to something else. Work — demanding, concentrated work — was her lifeline now.

All the same, she found it difficult to keep her mind on her job during that Friday afternoon when Kelita Holt had invited Lorne to her father's cocktail party. Had he accepted after all? Was he even now driving up to that mellow Cotswold house, bathed in golden sunshine, sharing champagne with her, taking her on to dinner afterwards?

Irritated with herself, Rachel threw a few things into her car and drove down to Exmoor to see her parents. Perhaps there she would find sanity. And relaxing for the next two days in their serene company, helping in the garden, walking on the moors, she did feel a good deal calmer. She drove back to Herefordshire on the Sunday evening feeling as if she had recovered from a temporary fever, scolding herself for having behaved like an infatuated teenager.

The Monday morning was warmer than ever. Rachel looked at her high-necked dresses and with a sudden impatient movement threw them back into the wardrobe. Why *should* she alter her style just because Lorne Quentin had made a few caustic remarks? In a mood of defiance, she took out a slim linen dress in rich cream, with a neckline that plunged between her breasts. She fastened a thin gold chain around her neck and slipped her feet into strappy sandals. The total effect was cool, composed and, she thought, a shade wicked. It summed up her mood exactly.

This morning, if Lorne were back — she

had a brief vision of him still with Kelita somewhere, maybe on that Bermudan island where her father owned a house! — she would show him that as far as she was concerned their relationship was purely business. If he couldn't keep his mind off sex, that was his problem. It wasn't up to her to stay under wraps simply because he couldn't control his own lustful feelings.

All right, so he hadn't made a pass the other night. But he'd dropped quite a few heavy hints that one was on the way. He'd left her flat that night just to increase her own desire — she'd worked that out over the weekend. Okay now *he* could do the wondering. And much good might it do him!

She wasn't about to make the same mistakes as she had before — start a relationship with a man who had his eyes on a bigger, wealthier prize. If Lorne Quentin intended marrying Kelita Holt, that was his own business. Rachel Grant did *not* intend to count as his final fling before doing so.

It grew hotter and hotter. The office was almost unnaturally quiet. Mike came in once, Penny twice. Rachel still didn't know whether Lorne had returned or not. She had just glanced at her watch to find it almost twelve when her phone rang.

With a sudden jump of her heart she lifted it, but it was Penny's voice which spoke. She sounded dubious and slightly anxious.

"Oh, Miss Grant, there's a man here to see Mr Quentin and he won't go. Mr Dalton and Mr Quentin are both in conference. I've told him that, and he says he wants to see you instead. It's something about a new design."

"A new design? You mean the Holt cars?" Rachel wondered why Penny was so flustered — surely she wouldn't have worried about anyone from Garfield.

"No, he's not from Holt's. He hasn't been here before at all. He's a Mr Marshall."

"Marshall?" Rachel flipped rapidly through her memory and could find no Marshall with whom the firm had dealings. "Well, all right, Penny, I'll see him. I seem to have got on top of the worst problem here." She tucked the phone under her chin and began to clear away a few papers from her desk. "Send him in, and if I want to get rid of him I'll refuse coffee in about ten minutes!"

A moment later the door opened and Penny appeared, still looking rather pink.

And behind her, to Rachel's astonishment, was a large young man. A man who reminded her immediately of a big, friendly bear; and who, on catching sight of her, gave a whoop of delight and rushed forwards, almost shouldering Penny out of the way and hauling Rachel out of her swivel chair to clasp her in an enthusiastic hug.

"Rachel! By all that's wonderful! I *wondered* if it could possibly be you. And look at all this — the splendour of it all!" He let her go and waved his arms expansively round the room, taking in her desk, her drawing-board, the big French windows and the view of the gardens.

"Ben!" Rachel gasped faintly. She caught sight of Penny hovering with wide, startled eyes in the doorway. "It's all right, Penny — Mr Marshall and I were at college together. And we'll have coffee right away, please — I've never known him to refuse a cup yet!"

Penny nodded and withdrew hastily, leaving Rachel and Ben Marshall holding each other by both hands. For a moment they stood quite still, examining each other's faces. Six years was a long time, Rachel thought, yet Ben didn't look any different. Bigger than ever, perhaps, and with a golden beard that made him look more like a Viking than a bear. But his eyes twinkled as much as ever and his face, tanned a deep golden-brown, didn't seem to have aged at all. She wondered what differences he was seeing in her.

Ben dropped her hands and began to move round the room.

"Sure, and you've done well for yourself here," he declared in the exaggerated Irish brogue that she remembered so well. "All this and a salary too! You must be making quite a name for yourself."

"Doing my best," Rachel said lightly. "And what about you? I haven't heard a word since we left college — what have you been up to?"

"Oh, this and that," he answered, and Rachel remembered that Ben had never been one of the most brilliant of the students in her year. Not that he couldn't have been but he was more often to be found organising a rag week or charity dance than studying. In those areas, he had shown a driving enthusiasm that his lecturers had coveted. "*Not* making a name for myself, evidently," he went on dryly. "No, darlin', you needn't look embarrassed, I didn't mean it like that. I haven't been one of the great army of unemployed, likely though it might seem." He glanced down at his clothes — open-necked shirt, corduroy trousers, light anorak. He might, she thought, have just come down from a mountain. He certainly didn't look like the usual kind of Quentin customer. But hadn't Penny said something about designs?

Ben nodded. "I'll come to that. I've been abroad most of the time since college — accounts for the rich tan — you thought I'd been idling on some Riviera beach, didn't you? Well, I haven't, and the tan's the only rich thing about me, I'm afraid." He paused as Penny came in with a tray of coffee. "I've been spending a lot of time in the Third World. India, mostly. And I've got a proposition to put to you — or, more accurately, to Quentin's. That's why I'm here." He turned suddenly and Rachel realised that his movements had been tense, jerky. Whatever this proposition was, it clearly meant a good deal to him. It would be easier for him to talk if he could be induced to relax. She indicated the chair opposite her own and poured the coffee.

"Sit down, Ben, you make the place look untidy. And have some coffee." She passed him a cup. "I just can't get over seeing you

181

here. It's marvellous. Tell me all about everything. Have you seen any of the others — Peter Watkins, and Sam?" They'd been his special cronies. "And Annette — do you ever hear anything of Annette these days?" Too late, she remembered that Ben and Annette had once seemed very close, and then everything had fallen apart. It had been only a month or two before they left college, and although she'd kept in casual contact with Annette, the other girl had never mentioned Ben again. But there was a shadow on Ben's face that seemed to indicate that it might have meant rather more to him.

"Yes, I've kept in touch with one or two," he said, omitting to mention Annette. "Peter Watkins, I saw him last week, he lives near my parents now. And I've had quite a lot to do with Beefy — remember Beefy Barron?" They both laughed. "I've never forgotten the time he and Sam got old Mugger's car on to the roof of the Buildings Department's classroom! They'd never let on how they did it, you know, Mugger nearly went mad."

"I remember." Rachel's eyes danced as she reminded him of another prank played by the same irrepressible couple, and they began to cap each other's stories, drawing out memories they hadn't known were still there. They were still roaring with laughter when Rachel caught sight of her wall-clock and discovered that it was almost one o'clock.

"Look at the time!" she exclaimed. "Ben, we haven't even started to talk about why you came. Look, why don't we go and have some lunch together and get all this nostalgia out of our systems, and then we'll come back and you can tell me just what you want Quentin's to do for you. Or do you want to do something for us? Never mind, we'll talk about it later." She gathered up her bag as she spoke and led the way out of the office, her shoulders already beginning to shake as a fresh memory invaded her. "Do you remember the time you and I —" she began, turning to Ben with eyes full of sparkling laughter and lips parted in the beginning of a smile. But the smile died on her lips and the laughter faded from her eyes. It wasn't Ben who stood immediately behind her. It was Lorne, who must have rounded the corner at the exact moment when she came through the door and who was now standing tall above her, looking down. His face was expressionless.

"Oh — Lorne!" she stammered, feeling

almost as guilty as if she'd actually been caught in some youthful prank. "I — I didn't know you were there."

"Evidently," he returned dryly, and let his glance move to Ben, who was still standing in the doorway.

"This — this is Ben Marshall, an old friend of mine from college," Rachel said rapidly, wondering why on earth she felt so embarrassed. She wasn't doing anything wrong, for heaven's sake! "Ben, this is Lorne Quentin. Lorne, Ben came to —"

"It's quite all right," Lorne said stiffly. "You don't have to explain your visitors to me, Rachel. And now, if you'll excuse me, I've got a business lunch. A rather important client." He passed Ben with a nod and went on down the corridor, leaving Rachel staring after him.

Temper rose inside her. How *could* he treat her like that? Like a naughty schoolgirl, caught out by teacher. Humiliating her in front of a potential client, even if he *hadn't* known that, had just thought of Ben as one of her previous boyfriends. And what if he were, would that matter at all to Lorne Quentin, who had shown her quite clearly that she was nothing to him, who hadn't even bothered to telephone her after their evening out?

Conscious of a touch of illogicality that only made her all the more cross, Rachel turned to Ben and pulled a face.

"Our illustrious employer," she said in a brittle voice. "He isn't always so rude. It must be a *very* important client. But you may feel you don't want to do business with Quentin's after all."

"No, I don't feel that." Ben's twinkling blue eyes rested thoughtfully on her face for a moment. "As you say, he's rather pre-occupied — perhaps he was late. And every client wants to feel he's important." They stood still for a moment, Rachel feeling oddly deflated, and then Ben touched her arm. "Let's go and have that lunch."

By the time they reached the car park, Rachel was laughing again, and as they stood by her car she let her head rest for a moment on Ben's shoulder in simple delight at being with him again, sharing memories that seemed now to be so young, so innocent — and so far away. There was an enormous comfort in having him here, big and real and uncomplicated, and she didn't want to let the feeling go.

But it all faded as she raised her head and found herself looking directly across the car park at Lorne Quentin and his companion. Lorne was looking straight back at her. And his 'important client' was none other than Kelita Holt.

Rachel was subdued as she drove Ben to the pub where they had lunch. But it didn't take her long to remind herself that whatever Lorne Quentin did was nothing to do with her — that she didn't *want* it to have anything to do with her. She turned her attention back to Ben, making a deliberate effort to regain her sparkle and delight in seeing him again, and by the time they returned to the office she was feeling more like her old self.

"Now then," she said, settling him in the largest armchair — Ben always looked too bulky to be comfortable in anything of normal size. "Tell me why you came here. And about your travels. We've done nothing but reminisce!"

"As it happens, they're very closely connected," Ben said, and his face was now serious. "I'm not here to buy a car, as such — but then you probably guessed that!" He paused, as if searching for words. "What I want is for you to build a car to my design — or to a design we can work out together based on my ideas. I know there are quite a few points I'll need help with, I never went much into car design, as you know. I was more of a general engineer. And this has to be a rather special sort of car. I'm afraid it won't bring you much profit."

Rachel looked at him, wondering what was in his mind. "Well, we could look at it," she said cautiously. "As a matter of fact, we're already doing something similar for another customer. Building a fleet of cars for his executives — prestige models that will become associated with both his name and ours. But I'm not sure we could —"

"No, you've got me wrong," he interrupted. "I'm not looking for prestige fleets, or a glossy image. And I don't have too much time. Nor do the people who'd be using the cars. But I would like Quentin to come in with me on this. Your cars are well-built and that's what I need. My design —"

"But we don't work to other people's designs," Rachel said. "We have our own design office. Why don't you tell us what you want and we'll work on your requirements."

"Would you? I wonder." His brown eyes were serious now as they watched her face. "Let's test it out, Rachel, shall we? I'll tell you what I want. I want a low-technology, low-cost car, built of epoxy-reinforced plywood, with wide-set wheels, high ground clearance, four-wheel drive, multi-speed gearbox and light suspension." He grinned at Rachel's expression. "And I only want you to produce a small, initial fleet — just prototypes. After that, I hope to get them built abroad."

Rachel stared at him. "What on earth — ? Ben, did you really say what I thought you said? A low-cost, low-technology, *plywood* —"

"And all the rest," he finished, still grinning. "Yes, that's what you heard. That's what I want. I've designed it, though as I say it probably wants a more professional eye cast over it for confirmation and improvements. And after the initial fleet, I doubt if you'd be required to build any more."

"But . . . I don't understand." Rachel passed her hand across her eyes. "What's it *for?* Why do you want us to build it? And why will you only a need a small fleet? Look, you'll have to tell me more."

"Gladly." He hitched his chair nearer the desk. "Look, I told you I've spent a lot of time in India. And there's a great need out there for a cheap, tough car that will travel over rough tracks and road, carrying a variety of people and equipment, with a low fuel consumption and the kind of construction that can be carried out with no more than the simple technology of a blacksmith's shop. The vehicles that are mostly in use — Land Rover types — just aren't right for the job. They're heavy, rigid, and cost a lot to import. My idea could make a considerable difference to both the economy and the way of life out there. A difference that's urgently needed."

Rachel stared at him, fascinated. When Penny put her head round the door to ask about tea, she nodded vaguely, and when her phone rang she said that she was taking no more calls that day as she was in an important meeting. At that, Ben sat back in his seat, and she realised that he must have been quite tense as he waited for her reaction.

"Look," she said as Penny brought the tea, "I'm interested in this idea, I can't pretend I'm not. But it's not my place to make a decision. I'm only Assistant Designer and Lorne Quentin himself has the overall say. You'll have to talk with him and Mike Dalton, the Chief Designer, about it."

"Oh yes," Ben Marshall said. "But you'll do that too, won't you? It would help to have you on my side. You see," he leaned forward, "this is really important. The Third World countries need all the help they can get, but they don't need it handed to them on a plate. This way, they can have the vehicles they need at low cost and produce them themselves. So it helps the economy in two ways, you see. Not only that, our vehicles just aren't suitable — they're made for modern, tarmac roads that in turn are expensive to build. It's a chicken and egg situation, but we can break through the shell by introducing the Indian T and —"

"What did you call it?" Rachel interrupted. "The Indian *what?*"

Ben Marshall looked shamefaced. "Indian T. All right, it's a bit of a joke, but it's just a working name. We can think of something better as we go along. The important thing is to get moving — get a firm interested, get production started. Then we can enter the car for some really tough, publicity-catching rallies and endurance tests to prove it will work, and get the Indian authorities to agree to production. But it needs to be done quickly. There are people out there who can't wait."

Rachel thought of TV news programmes she'd seen about the problems faced by Third World countries — problems of drought or famine, inevitably exacerbated by the difficulties of getting supplies across almost impossible terrain to those most desperately in need of them. Would the Indian T be able to help in such situations? And the economy too, which needed a vital injection of industry — industry that would be of some use to the countries involved, give men jobs they could feel a pride in, producing something real and necessary rather than the paper flowers and cheap ornaments that made her feel ashamed when she saw them in charity shops. Was this car the answer, or, at least, the beginning of an answer? A bubble of excitement rose inside her as she looked at Ben Marshall. There was no doubting his sincerity or his enthusiasm. And it was infectious. She *wanted* to work with him on this, and not just because he was an old friend.

She leaned over her desk, eyes green and sparkling.

"All right," she said, ignoring the warning voice inside that told her she ought to pass this directly to Lorne. "Let me see your plans. And then," she glanced quickly at her watch, "good lord, it's nearly five! Where are you staying, Ben?"

"Oh, I haven't bothered about that yet — didn't know if I'd need to be staying anywhere! Don't worry, I'll find somewhere in Hereford."

"You most certainly will not. There's a spare bed at my cottage and you're more than welcome to it." Her eyes glowed. "It'll be like old times, Ben, you and me, talking far into the night. And the plans — I don't think I've been so excited about anything for years!"

She was leaning forward as she spoke, her bright hair almost touching Ben's, her eyes smiling into his, one hand extended towards him. Her back was to the French window; it was only Ben's expression and some change in the light that warned her there was someone there, standing just outside the open door able to hear every word. Slowly, she turned round.

"It's good to know that you're enjoying your work so much," Lorne said formally. "I'm only surprised to find you still here. Don't you and Mr Marshall want to get away and continue your, er, reminiscences in private?" His eyes were like slate as he regarded Rachel, and the temperature of the room seemed to drop by at least ten degrees. "Don't delay on my account, or by any minor thing such as working hours."

Ben rose clumsily to his feet and held out a big hand. "I'm sorry, Mr Quentin — I know how it must look to you. But I came here with a business proposition — I didn't even know Rachel was working here. I'd like to talk to you as well, if I may — it's about a car I've designed and —"

"It's kind of you to think of us," Lorne interrupted, his voice like ice, "but as I'm sure Rachel has explained to you — or will as soon as she remembers it — we don't use other people's designs. We have our own team." His cold eyes rested briefly on Rachel's burning face. "Or at least, I thought we had. But perhaps she hasn't got around to telling you that, either. In which case, I won't take up any more of your time." He turned back to the window, saying curtly to Rachel: "I'd be glad if you could come in fairly early tomorrow. I've several points I want to discuss with you. Provided it doesn't interfere with your own plans, of course." Another brief flicker of a glance at Ben, and he was gone.

"Well!" Rachel exploded as soon as he was out of sight. "The *swine!*"

Ben grinned. "Just exerting his authority

as an employer," he said. "Or maybe there's something else between you. Could it have been a flash of the old green-eyed monster I saw peeping from those cool grey eyes just then?"

"It most certainly couldn't!" Rachel cursed her pale skin, that flushed so easily. "There's nothing between Lorne Quentin and me, nor could there ever be. He just wanted to be unpleasant and upset me. And it's not going to work!" she finished furiously.

Ben laughed outright. "No? If you say so!" His eyes twinkled and she gave him a shamefaced grin. All right, so her outburst *had* been a little heated, but he'd remember her occasional flashes of temper from college days. He wouldn't read anything into that. And her main concern was that she shouldn't have ruined any chance of Lorne considering Ben's plans. "Are you going to stay the night?" she asked. "I'd like you to."

"And I'd like to, very much, as long as it doesn't cause any gossip. Don't want to ruin your reputation."

"Oh, for heaven's sake, this is the nineteen-nineties, isn't it? People don't think like that any more. And look, let me see Lorne alone about your designs tomorrow.

It might be better if I grovel a bit — on your behalf, of course." She wouldn't be doing any such thing for her own benefit! "You can go and have a look at Hereford. It's an interesting little place. Old black and white buildings, narrow, cobbled streets, a big, red sandstone cathedral with a Chained Library going back to before William the Conqueror. Or if you feel energetic, go and have a walk in the Black Mountains, they're not far away."

"I like the sound of both ideas," Ben said, giving her a quizzical glance. "But I'm not here on holiday, you know. Wouldn't it be better if I came and saw Quentin myself?"

Rachel hesitated. She felt strongly that it wouldn't, but she was unable to say clearly why. Even if she and Ben pored over the plans until late that night — as they probably would — he would still be able to give the best explanation of what he wanted. But she had a disquieting feeling that seeing her and Ben together had an oddly inflammatory effect on Lorne.

"I just think it'd be better if I broached the subject on my own," she said lamely. "You heard what he said — he's quite capable of refusing to see you at all. But he ought at least to listen to me, as his Assistant Designer. And it *is* pretty revolutionary, even for Quentin's. I honestly don't think he's going to jump at it. He'll need persuading." She coloured, unable to help thinking that Ben would be justified in doubting her persuasive ability where Lorne was concerned.

"That's just why I came to Quentin's, because it's unconventional," Ben said. "But all right, Rachel, if you think it's best. I'll take myself off somewhere for the day. And we'd better spend the evening going into detail." He looked rueful. "I'd planned to take you out to dinner, but that won't leave us much time. Let's make it a date for tomorrow evening, shall we? A celebration, or a commiseration, whichever it turns out to be."

"A celebration," Rachel said firmly, and wished she felt as confident as she sounded.

Her words came back to her next day as she drove into the car park behind Quentin Court. This had once, she supposed, been the stableyard; she sat for a moment looking at the old house, built in local red sandstone, and wondering what feelings Lorne had for it. Did he ever regret the long-lost days when this house had been

196

the focal point of the whole area, managing a large estate with perhaps a dozen or more tenant farms, and half the villages in the district working in some way for the family who lived there? Did he resent the fact that the grounds now housed a factory, however well-concealed, and that the major part of the house itself was given over to offices, canteens, a social centre? He still had his own apartment there, and Rachel wondered as she made her way to her own pleasant office, just what it was like. She had never been invited into the part that was Lorne's home; he was, she realised, an essentially private man. Did he find all this an intrusion, or did he never even think of it in that way? He'd been accustomed to it since he was a child, after all.

For some reason, her mind went back to the evening — was it really so short a time ago? — which they had spent together, when she had told Lorne about her childhood and asked him about his. His reply had been brief, even brusque. Less than idyllic, he'd said, and reeled off a few staccato phrases which had left her with the impression of a chilly, almost loveless boyhood. Was that the reason for his apparent reluctance to become deeply involved with women, to keep them at arm's length? Wasn't it true that men who had never had proper relationships with their mothers grew up unable to form them with other women?

Rachel caught herself up. What on earth was she doing, musing like this about Lorne? Half-baked psychology, she told herself. You know nothing really about Lorne Quentin and what makes him tick. Forget the man except as an employer. He's nothing else to you, never has been, never can be. And you don't even want him to be, in spite of this crazy physical attraction. So stop it!

Having given herself this little pep-talk, she walked boldly into Lorne's outer office and told Julie she was ready to see him. "He asked me to come in early," she added, "and I've got a few things to discuss with him myself."

"Yes, he told me to keep the morning free." Julie lifted her telephone and told Lorne that Rachel was here. "Go on in."

Rachel walked through the door, conscious of a quickening heartbeat. What was Lorne's attitude going to be this morning — the icy formality he'd displayed yesterday, the easy-going friendliness he'd shown her when they'd been out together

198

— or a touch of the tenderness he'd revealed as they said good-night? *Most* unlikely, she thought ruefully, and braced herself to meet cold grey eyes and a forbiddingly grim mouth.

But Lorne seemed to have decided upon an impersonal remoteness, treating her as if she were of no more importance to him than a shop assistant. He was sitting at his desk, going through some post, and he glanced up only to wish her a cool good-morning and invite her to sit down before going back to his letters.

Rachel sat down, inwardly seething. But there was nothing she could say. If Lorne liked to pay her a high salary to sit and watch him read letters, that was his affair. Her time, while at the office, was his. All the same, she couldn't help a simmering resentment at being treated in such a way.

At last Lorne looked up and laid his letters to one side. His eyes rested on her, thoughtful and enigmatic. How long would it take, Rachel wondered, for a woman to learn to read Lorne Quentin accurately? Could it be done at all? And what sort of woman would she have to be?

"You're looking tired," Lorne said unexpectedly. "I suppose you had a late night last night. It must have been quite a

199

change for you, having your . . . friend . . . visiting."

"It was," Rachel answered stiffly. "A very pleasant change. I haven't seen Ben for some time." She'd been going to say 'years' but changed her mind at the last moment. Why should she tell Lorne anything? 'Some time' could be anything — years, months, even weeks — depending on how she felt about Ben. Let Lorne think what he liked!

"So I gathered." His eyes moved over her slowly. As if he were looking for traces of — what? A night's heavy love-making? Some tiny devil inside prompted her not to disillusion him.

"It never seems to matter how long we've been apart, though," she added with what she hoped was a reminiscent smile. "Ben and I always seem to be able to pick up and carry on just as if we'd been together all the time."

She gave Lorne a smile that invited him to understand more than she'd actually said. His lips tightened and she had a sudden stab of remorse. *Not* the most sensible of moves, she told herself. He'd clearly taken her point all too well, and equally clearly he didn't like it. That male ego of his, which liked to be the sole focus of female attention! Now he'd be automatically against any plan that Ben might offer, and just because of a mischievous impulse on her part. Well, there was nothing she could do about it now.

"I didn't actually ask you here to discuss your social life," Lorne said coldly, just as if he hadn't broached the subject. "As I said, there are one or two points I want to go over regarding Garfield's order. I'd have liked to discuss them yesterday, but you were otherwise engaged. But we can get through them this morning — that's if you've no further appointments?" Again, his cold eyes raked her and Rachel felt her cheeks colour as she murmured that she was quite free. Together, they moved over to the table where Lorne had laid out the designs.

Rachel bent her head, part of her mind listening to Lorne as he explained the points he'd wanted to make, while the other was acutely conscious of his nearness, the way his arm brushed against hers, the way the soft tendrils of her hair touched his cheek. Quite clearly, he wasn't in the least affected by her; his voice remained smooth, his fingers traced steady lines on the papers. With a sudden movement, Rachel shifted away from him and was aware of his curious glance on her before he went on with what he was saying.

"Well, that seems to be it for now," he said at last, straightening up. "I think we deserve a cup of coffee, don't you?" He touched Julie's buzzer and spoke into the intercom. "Was there anything else you wanted to say?"

Now was the moment. "Yes," she said, "as a matter of fact there was. Not about Garfield's cars, though. It was something quite different. It's about Ben."

She saw Lorne's muscles stiffen under the thin cotton of his shirt, but his voice was casual. "Ben? The large, hairy young Viking you had here yesterday?"

"That's right." *Don't let him needle you.* "Ben Marshall. I told you, we were at college together, and he brought an idea for a design he's —"

"I remember," Lorne interrupted. "And I think I told him we had our own design team." His eyes glinted at her. "That's right, isn't it, Rachel? You do consider yourself part of my team?"

"Yes — yes, of course," Rachel stammered. "But you don't understand what Ben's doing — what he wants is —"

"He wants to sell us a design, I know."

Lorne's voice was bored. "Rachel, I quite see that you haven't been with us long enough to have encountered this kind of thing before, but it happens quite regularly, you know. A keen young design engineer, probably unemployed, hawks his ideas round all the car manufacturers in the hope that one of them will either buy his work or give him a job. It isn't in the least unusual, but you have to learn to spot them and not let them waste your time. If it happens again, refer them to me, I've a way with them."

"But it wasn't like that at all! Ben had a real proposition to make —"

"So do they all."

"His design is something quite unusual."

"I can believe that, too!"

"Oh, you won't even listen, will you!" Rachel cried. She stopped as Julie came in with the coffee, then went on more calmly. "Just give me ten minutes to explain, Lorne, please. If you're not interested after that, I'll tell Ben to take his ideas elsewhere. He doesn't have any more time to mess about than you do — what he's doing is *important*."

"And what I'm doing isn't?" Lorne sat down, poured coffee and leaned back. "All right. Ten minutes."

Rachel took a deep breath. Lorne meant it, she knew that. If she hadn't got Ben's ideas across successfully in ten minutes, it would be no go. She spoke quickly, positively, determined to convince him.

"It's this new car he wants us to build," she said. "He's designed it himself — something absolutely different — low-technology, four-wheel drive, high ground clearance, built of reinforced plywood. It's for the —"

"*What* did you say?" Lorne put down his cup and stared at her. "Rachel, what on earth are you talking about?"

"I told you, Ben's designed this car he wants us to build —"

"He wants *us* to build to *his* design? I hope you told him that was out, for a start!"

"No, I didn't. He understands that we'd probably modify the design quite a bit — it's just a first draft, as it were. Lorne, you don't understand. This is something quite out of the ordinary and —"

"I rather gathered that! Did I actually hear you say something about *plywood?* Rachel, the man's out of his mind. He's a crank, a lunatic, and so must you be to have listened to him — and to come to me with this faradiddle." He shook his head, wonderingly. "And to think that I gave you credit for quite a lot of sense!"

Rachel felt a cold tongue of anger lick at her mind. "Ben is perfectly sensible," she said coldly. "Unconventional, perhaps, but —"

"You can say that again," Lorne broke in, and Rachel wondered briefly if he would ever let her finish a sentence without interruption. How *could* she explain properly when he wouldn't even listen? But she kept a tight hold on her temper; she'd already lessened Ben's chances and she wasn't going to ruin them completely. "You'd have to be unconventional to build plywood cars," Lorne went on sarcastically. "Just what is the purpose of this vehicle, anyway? Some sort of toy, a rival to that electric three-wheeler that caused so much fuss? And why on earth did he come to us? Because he knew you, I suppose."

"Ben had no idea I was working here. He came, presumably, because he thought he might get a sympathetic hearing — from *you*. Obviously he was wrong. And the purpose of this vehicle is to provide cheap transport as well as industry for the Third World. It's not a toy at all. He wants us to build a few prototypes so that he can show the Indian Government what he has in mind. Then they can build them there instead of importing expensive European cars that aren't built for the job anyway, and —"

"Well, he certainly got you pretty thoroughly brainwashed," Lorne remarked. "I wonder you haven't turned over the entire production line to this — what does he call it?"

"The Indian T." Rachel answered reluctantly, and Lorne gave a hoot of laughter.

"The *Indian T?* Oh, I'm sorry, Rachel, but just what kind of a guy *is* this Ben Marshall? Some sort of a joker? You seemed to think he was pretty funny yesterday. Is he really serious about this?"

"Yes, he is," Rachel answered simply. "I've known Ben for a long time, and he *is* a joker — about little, everyday things. He gets a lot of fun out of life. But not out of things like the Third World." She met Lorne's eyes. "He's been out in India ever since he left college — went on voluntary service overseas, and stayed. He knows what he's talking about, Lorne. And he's very serious indeed."

Lorne was silent for a moment, watching her face. Then he nodded slightly. "All right, Rachel," he said quietly. "Tell me all about it. Then I'll tell you whether I think this Ben of yours is a crank or a joker. And this time I won't interrupt."

At last, she thought, and took another deep breath to control the shaking of her voice as she told him all that she and Ben had discussed the day before. As she spoke, her shaking ceased and enthusiasm took over; by the time she finished her eyes were alight and her voice excited as she described the difference this could make to the poorest areas of India, in both their economy and their transport difficulties. In her mind, she saw convoys of trucks, all made from Ben's basic design, carrying food and clothing to areas struck by famine or floods; school buses taking children from outlying areas to school; lorries transporting essential equipment to villages that were still living in the Stone Age . . .

Lorne's first words brought her sharply back to earth.

"It won't work."

Rachel gave her head a little shake, almost in bewilderment at finding herself still in the pleasant office with the sound of birds singing in the garden outside. For a few moments she had been out in India with Ben, working to alleviate the suffering of thousands of impoverished people. "What?" she said blankly.

"It won't work. No go. Completely out of the question."

Her visions faded. She stared at him, seeing nothing but a stony face, granite eyes. "You mean you won't even consider it?"

"I don't have to! Look, the whole idea's too way-out. Plywood cars! What makes this Ben Marshall think that plywood is low-technology? He talks about building in a local blacksmith's shop or boatyard — the average Indian village blacksmith isn't going to be able to put together a plywood car, no way! And where's the plywood going to come from? Has he thought of that? That's technology in itself. As for low-cost, since when have four-wheel drive and eight-speed gearboxes been low-cost? I'm sorry, Rachel, but I just don't see how your friend Ben *can* be serious over this. Not if he's any kind of engineer at all."

Rachel was silent. Reluctant though she was to admit it, her own professional knowledge told her that Lorne was right. But Ben *had* trained as an engineer — surely he wouldn't have made elementary mistakes in something as important to him — to the world — as this. She cast her

208

mind back to their college days and found she wasn't actually too clear about Ben's abilities, he'd been much more prominent on the social scene. And since then, had he actually worked as an engineer? Rachel was hazy about voluntary service overseas, but he could have been doing almost anything.

All the same, she'd been impressed by his sincerity, his enthusiasm and the amount of work he obviously had put into his project, and she didn't want to let the idea go just like that. Wasn't Lorne being just a little too quick to dismiss it?

"Are you sure you're not just making excuses?" she asked stubbornly. "All right, I agree with some of the points you've just made, but not all of them. I think Ben's idea *is* viable, with some modifications, which he's perfectly prepared for. It won't be profitable, of course. Perhaps that's what's really putting you off?" She grasped at the idea, her voice rising a little as she developed it. "Yes, that's it. There's no money in low-cost technology, in helping some poor underprivileged country to help itself, is there? Sell them expensive modern cars totally unsuited to the environment, yes — if you got an order for a fleet from a raja or an oil-sheikh, that would be a very different story. But show them how to build their own —"

"And now you're just being hysterical," Lorne said wearily. "Look, Rachel, you're an experienced engineer, you understand the problems as well as I do. Yes, it might well be possible to modify Marshall's original idea. But is Quentin's the firm to do it? Do we even have the time, the capacity? I'm not at all sure. And without going into it a lot more deeply, I've no intention of saying anything further." He finished his coffee; Rachel hadn't even started hers. "Now, we've taken up enough time this morning. I want something settled about those points on Garfield's designs by tomorrow, and then you can go over and see him. He doesn't need to see me again at this stage." He glanced at her as she stood without moving before his desk. "Well, go along then, Rachel. I've got an appointment in five minutes."

Rachel turned on her heel and marched stiffly from the room. So Lorne was intransigent. He'd turned Ben's plans down out of hand. He intended to have nothing to do with them.

Unexpected tears burned her eyes, yet she had to admit that, deep down, she'd expected nothing else. Lorne had been hardly likely to commit his firm to branch out into an entirely new field, into something so revolutionary, something that could be almost guaranteed to make a loss rather than the profits they needed to survive. There wasn't really any reason for her to be surprised, even resentful.

It was just that she had an idea there was more to Lorne's refusal than plain economics — something more personal. And it would have been so rewarding to do something that wasn't, for once, entirely bound up with profit. Something that one could feel proud of in a way that had nothing to do with commercial success. Ben's enthusiasm had been infectious, and Rachel was feeling now almost as disappointed as he must when she told him the news later.

It was only then that she remembered that she had left the plans in Lorne's office. But when she went back to recover them, Julie told her that Lorne's next visitor had already arrived and he'd given strict instructions that he wasn't to be disturbed. She would have to try again later.

Rachel went back to her own room. She couldn't help wondering who Lorne's important visitor was. A supplier? A new customer? Some celebrity who had decided that a Quentin car would be his next symbol of success?

Or maybe it was the same 'important client' he'd taken to lunch yesterday — Kelita Holt, the teenage *femme fatale* who had shown herself so determined to fasten her pretty red claws into him, and who was going to end up either as Mrs Lorne Quentin or very badly hurt.

You've got no reason to suppose it's Kelita, Rachel told herself sternly, and it's no business of yours anyway. You're just stupidly, ridiculously obsessed. And at your age, you should know better.

So why didn't she?

Seven

Rachel was distracted and thoughtful as she drove over to Garfield Holt's Cotswold home a few days later. Suddenly, everything seemed to be happening at once — both at work and in that private life which seemed to go on mostly in her head, where Lorne Quentin appeared to dominate her thoughts. She sighed with exasperation. Hadn't she decided that her feelings for him were merely an infatuation — a pretty powerful one, admittedly, but then Lorne's attraction *was* powerful, by any standards. And maybe she was just over-reacting, something to do with her leaving Britton's, breaking free from her old life, and having spent the last few years in a kind of shell.

Her normal instincts were just reawakening, that was it. And, like a girl newly become a woman, she was vulnerable to any attractive man. Unlike a young girl, however, she could recognise the phenomenon for what it was and know that it would pass. Eventually.

Just stop thinking about him so much,

she advised herself. Stop picturing that slow smile, the way his eyes turn silver and crinkle at the corners, the way he made you feel when he kissed you. Just stop *thinking* about the way he kissed you . . .

There was no reason, no reason at all why one man should dominate and completely take over the thoughts of a capable, sophisticated, liberated career woman like herself. One man — no different from millions of other men . . .

Except that Lorne *was* different. And Rachel was clearly neither so sophisticated nor so liberated as she liked to believe.

Well, today she would forget him for a while. Garfield Holt was waiting to discuss his new fleet of cars, and while they did that she could keep Lorne in his place as employer and businessman. Without him present, maybe she could forget his disturbing vitality.

Rachel frowned, her thoughts turning to Ben and his own design. She'd hated going back to the cottage the other evening and seeing his hopeful, expectant face, watching the eagerness die from it as she'd told him Lorne's reactions. "I'm really sorry," she'd said, leaning across the table to take his hands. "I did all I could. And he didn't actually give me a definite no. But I honestly don't think there's any hope." She lifted her briefcase and took out the plans she'd recovered from Lorne's office just before leaving work. To her relief, he hadn't been there and she'd just picked them up from the table and slipped out without seeing him. "I'm sorry, Ben," she said again, helplessly.

"Well, you tried," he said, making an attempt to hide his disappointment. "I'll just have to go somewhere else, I suppose. There must be *someone* who'd take up the idea." His voice was dejected, and Rachel sighed and stood up. It was time to start preparing a meal.

"I'm sure there will be. You'll get a backer, Ben, I'm sure you will. I just wish it could have been us. I'd have jumped at the chance of working on a project like that."

They talked of other things as Rachel grilled the fresh trout Ben had brought home from a fish farm he'd passed during the day. He stood at the sink, washing lettuce and slicing tomatoes; big, comfortable, easy to be with. Rachel cut up some fruit and mixed it together in a glass bowl with orange juice and *Grand Marnier*. Why couldn't it be like this between her and Lorne? she wondered sadly. Easy, comfortable, with no painful tensions. She swept up the fruit peelings and dropped them in the waste-bin. She would *not* think about Lorne!

Before leaving for work that morning, she had put a bottle of white wine into the refrigerator. She took it out now and they carried everything out into the little garden, setting it on the old white-painted iron table that had been there when she moved in. The air was still warm, the sun low in the sky and partially hidden by a web of thin golden cloud. A thrush sang loudly from the branches of an ancient apple tree and other birds joined in, twittering and fussing as they roosted for the night.

"There's something I want to tell you, Rachel," Ben said abruptly as they began to eat. She looked at him enquiringly. He sounded unusually serious — not surprising when he'd just had his designs turned down, but she had a feeling he wasn't thinking about them now.

"It's not about the car," he said, confirming her intuition. "At least, only indirectly. It's something you asked me yesterday." He took a sip of wine. "You asked me about Annette."

"Yes, and you said you didn't hear much

216

from her now." Rachel watched him curiously. "Wasn't it true?"

"Well, no, not entirely. In a way, it was — a purely literal way." He gave her an apologetic glance. "I don't hear from her much — I see her. Quite a lot, actually."

"You see her? You mean, you and Annette —" Rachel broke off, unsure just how to put it. Clearly, Ben and Annette were involved in some way, but how deeply? And why hadn't he said so straightaway?

"We just see each other," Ben repeated. "There isn't any more to it than that. We don't live together, we're not engaged, we're not having an affair." He gave her a wry look. "Any one of those would suit me, for starters anyway. But Annette won't have it."

"Well . . ." Rachel gestured helplessly. "There doesn't seem to be much you can do about it, then."

"Oh, there is," he said gloomily. "There is. I've got to *achieve* something, you see. That's her stipulation. She says I'm lazy. Oh yes, she knows about India, but that doesn't make any difference. And she's right. I just drifted out there, doing whatever came to hand, helping with whatever needed doing. There was plenty, so it was easy. That's the whole point, it was *easy* to help. There's such a lot to do. I could work as hard as the next man, and as long hours, and I did. I told myself I was being of real use. But Annette won't have it. She says I wasn't using myself properly. I wasn't working to my full potential, stretching myself. I was only doing what hundreds of other people could do, instead of what only *I* could do."

Rachel listened, fascinated. Annette had said something very similar to herself, she remembered. Made her see that she had something to give, and not to give it wasn't merely stupid, it was downright immoral. Burying your talents, she'd called it, and gone on to say that it was no use waiting to be asked — unless Rachel displayed her talents nobody would even know she had them. Make the best of yourself, she'd urged, stretch to your full potential as a woman — and a person. And it had worked. Annette's strategy hadn't just given Rachel confidence in her own femininity — a confidence which had never left her, even through the pain of Graham's betrayal — it had made her sure of herself professionally as well.

"So what does she want you to do?" she asked Ben, and as soon as the words were out she knew the answer. "Oh — the car."

"The car. Annette thinks it's the greatest idea since cornflakes, but she knows that if I don't get someone to accept it I'll just go tamely back to India and keep on slogging away like I did before." He glanced down at his plate, adding quietly in a way that brought a sudden sting to Rachel's eyes: "I'm really involved out there, you see. It's where I want to be. It's my life, I suppose. But, well, Annette thinks I'm capable of more, and I want to prove her right."

"And she *is* right," Rachel exclaimed warmly. "You *can* do something really useful with your life. This car could be only a beginning."

"Well," he said, "there you are. I just wanted to tell you about it, Rachel."

"And what happens if you get this project on the road? If someone takes up your idea and gets the Indian T going into production? Will Annette live with you? Get engaged? Have an affair?"

"We'll get married," Ben said simply, and Rachel caught the unfamiliar tone in his voice and knew that this was the most important — and the most unattainable — desire in his world.

Driving now through Tewkesbury and turning the nose of her car towards the blue Cotswold hills, she pictured them together. Ben, big, comforting, utterly dependable, and Annette, tiny and fragile as a fairy, full of life and strength, determined to bring out of Ben the enormous reserve that still lay hidden. And she would do it, Rachel felt certain. She would help him to fulfil himself, to realise his own potential, and all without yielding one scrap of her own lively personality. There would be no dominant factor in their relationship, just two partners. If only there were something she could do to help.

Rachel wished that she'd been able to persuade Ben to stay longer, but he'd shaken his head. "There isn't really much point, much as I'd like to," he said. "I've got to make an effort, try a few other manufacturers." But he didn't sound enthusiastic; he had pinned his hopes on Quentin's. "But we won't lose touch again. I'll bring Annette to see you sometime. She often talks about you and wonders how you're getting on."

"Yes, you do that, and make it soon." Rachel watched him leave, feeling as if part of her past was going with him. They had been happy days at college, happier than they'd realised at the time, with only exams to worry about and few responsibilities. Now, they were all out in the real world, coping with problems that often seemed almost insurmountable. Ben with his car, herself with her feelings for Lorne. Would they ever look back and wonder what they'd worried about?

Ben's visit had been a fiasco, and Rachel still had an uncomfortable feeling that it had been largely her fault. If she and Ben hadn't seemed so intimate . . . But that couldn't have made any real difference, surely? Lorne was too professional to let the fact that Ben was her friend interfere with a business proposition. Not that there was any reason why it should — he'd made it plain enough that he had no personal feelings about her.

All right, so he'd kissed her. Twice. Once with a passion that still shook her whenever she allowed herself to think about it; and once with a tenderness that somehow had an even more profound effect.

But those kisses hadn't meant a thing to *him*. That was what she had to remember.

Garfield Holt was waiting for her when she drove up to the long, low house. It was looking even more beautiful this morning, she thought, like a huge golden cat drowsing contentedly in the summer sunshine. Life itself ought to be contented in a house like this — uncomplicated, simple; a long, comfortable holiday. But she dismissed the thought at once, knowing that such a life would never really suit her. She enjoyed her work too much, needed it as an outlet for her restless, creative energy. If she lived in a house like this and had no work, what would she do? What every other countrywoman did, of course — join in the local community, fill her days with village interests, garden, cook, bring up a family . . .

Rachel got out of the car and smiled at Garfield as he came forward to greet her. She had come to like the bluff businessman at their earlier meeting, suspecting hidden depths beneath that tough exterior. Quite obviously he wouldn't have reached his present position without a good deal of shrewd toughness, but something else had looked out of his eyes once or twice, especially when he'd spoken of his dead wife. Something essentially simple and oddly touching; something that went with this dreaming landscape.

"There you are, Rachel my dear." She noticed with an inward smile that he'd decided to take up Kelita's suggestion that they should all be on first-name terms. "Glad to see you. Lovely morning, isn't it?" His rather small, dark eyes looked around the lush meadows spread out below the house, at trees heavy with foliage, at cows knee-deep in the long grass. "The kind of morning when it's good to be in the countryside. I've been in London all this week — get tired of the city life sometimes, you know, wonder why I ever let myself get caught up in the rat-race. But there it is, it's in my blood now and I don't suppose I'll ever leave it." He put his hand under her arm to guide her into the house. "I've been over those designs with some of my colleagues and they've come up with one or two new ideas, I don't know if they'll be any good. Just small points. And you've brought me Lorne's ideas, is that right?"

"Yes, we had a discussion about them a few days ago and I've been working on them. I don't think you'll find any problems there." She wondered what the new ideas were. Just small points, Garfield said, but when non-engineers started to have their own ideas it could often mean a complete rethink on the basics. Even more often, they were completely impractical.

"Good, good." Garfield led her through to the cool sitting-room and gave her a tall, frosty glass of ice-cold lemonade. "Thought you might appreciate a cool drink after your drive. Mrs Appleby makes it and I always say there's nothing like it on a hot day. Or would you rather have something stronger?"

"No, no, this is lovely." Rachel sipped the refreshing liquid. Garfield was evidently in no hurry to start their discussion. She wandered over to the open French windows and stood looking out at the shady terrace. A table stood there with some chairs and sun-loungers. Garfield came to stand beside her.

"I thought we might have a spot of lunch out here," he suggested. "It's a pity I didn't think of it, you could have brought your swimming-costume and had a bathe. The pool's just beyond the terrace, see?" He glanced at her figure. "I wonder if Kelita's left any of her costumes here. They ought to fit you."

"Oh, no," Rachel protested at once, "I couldn't wear anything of Kelita's — not without asking her, anyway. And I don't really feel like swimming today, though it's a nice idea — I'll come prepared next time." She followed him out to the terrace and saw the pool, set in a sheltered walled garden, surrounded by flowering shrubs. "It's lovely, really beautiful." Had Lorne ever bathed here? she wondered. Perhaps after that cocktail party? Perhaps when he'd taken Kelita to lunch the day Ben came to the factory. Perhaps after a dinner out somewhere; she imagined the pool, lit by the soft glow of the moon, a perfect rendezvous for romance.

"I thought you'd like it," Garfield said, pouring another drink. "I've noticed you seem to like the whole house. That's nice. Kelita doesn't like it, not really. She's a city girl — feels uneasy away from the bright lights and roar of traffic." He handed Rachel her drink and offered her a chair under a small weeping-willow. "You're more like my wife used to be. In fact," he hesitated, "you remind me of my wife more than Kelita ever does. You like the simple pleasures of life, just like she did."

Rachel gave him a quick, startled glance but he was staring at the pool as if he were somewhere else. She felt a pang of com-passion. Garfield Holt was, as she'd thought on her previous visit, essentially a loving and lonely man. He'd tried hard to replace his dead wife with his daughter, and he was beginning to realise now that it hadn't worked — couldn't work. However close they were, a daughter couldn't be to her father what a wife would be. The time would come when she must leave him to live her own life. Kelita had already done that, to all intents and purposes. She quite clearly considered her life her own affair, her father with his beautiful Cotswold house, and home in London, merely a base. It wouldn't be too long before she wanted complete independence — her own flat, an allowance sufficient to provide all her wants. Rachel doubted whether Garfield would see much of his daughter once that had been achieved.

"I wouldn't call this one of the simple pleasures of life," she said with a little laugh, glancing round at their surroundings.

"Oh, but it is really. Sitting in the shade on a summer's day, drinking something pleasant — and home-made, none of your fancy stuff — looking at the water; what could be simpler than that? And sharing it with someone you like — that makes it all the better. Puts the finishing touches on it, you might say." He paused, then said a little huskily, his accent more noticeable than usual: "I haven't really had anyone to share things with since my wife died." There was a moment's silence, then he lifted his head and said in a brisk tone: "But I'm getting to sound sorry for myself, and that won't do. I flatter myself I don't bother others with my problems — like I said before, you've got a sympathetic face. You're easy to talk to. Anyway," he levered himself from his chair, "let's go in and look at these designs, get that out of the way before lunch. Else you'll be thinking I've got you over here on false pretences."

They went in to the study and Rachel went over the designs with him, showing him Lorne's modifications and explaining the reasons for them. To her relief, the ideas put forward by Garfield's colleagues were easy to incorporate — they weren't really basic design ideas at all, just small additions and embellishments to the inside features of the car, concerned with style rather than function. She made a few notes, then folded the plans and smiled at her host.

"That's it, then. I'll go back and work on stage two. It shouldn't take too long to get everything settled, and then we can schedule production."

"Good. I'm very pleased with the way things are going." Garfield looked at his watch. "Now, Mrs Apppleby was going to put us a cold buffet out on the terrace, and it should be ready now. We'll forget work for a while, shall we? Relax — get to know each other a bit better."

He led the way out to the terrace, where the table was now spread with an assortment of cold meats and salads, all kept cool by a bed of ice in which the platters and bowls rested. Rachel helped herself to a selection, poured another tall glass of fresh lemonade and sat down.

"What lovely salad," she said. "Do you grow your own vegetables here?"

"Oh yes, there's quite a large kitchen garden. Appleby looks after it mostly, but I must admit I take a few hours off now and then and get out there too with a hoe and a fork." Garfield sat down beside her. "It's a grand thing — makes me feel like an ordinary man for a few hours. My old dad was that, you know — just an ordinary working man. Used to work in a factory in Birmingham. We lived in a terraced house, two-up and two-down — six of us, all on top of each other. Poor as church mice, you see. But we never went hungry. We had a bit of garden and we grew our own vegetables and had a little run with some hens in so we could have our own eggs. I used to like helping out in the garden — thought at one time I might take it up, get a job with the local council in the park or something of that. Ah, they were good days, taking it all round. We worked hard, didn't have much, but we had something that seems to be missing now. I dunno. I thought it was maybe to do with there being four of us kids, a real family if you take my meaning, but it's hard to know, really." He paused for a moment, far away in his thoughts. "I used to go and stay with my grandparents in the country during the summer holidays, too. I was a bit sickly as a lad, and the doctor said fresh air'd do me good. Seems like summer all the time, now I think back. We used to go blackberrying, us kids, bring back great basketfuls, and my gran'd make them into pies and jam. I'd take a few pots home for the family and we'd have them for Sunday tea. And mushrooms, we'd get up early in the mornings and gather 'em before anyone else got the chance. Went lovely with a bit of bacon and an egg." He sighed. "Better than all your fancy meals. Things don't have the taste these days — everything's too refined." He seemed to come back to himself and gave her a quick, half-apologetic look. "I'm sorry, Rachel, I'm going on, aren't I? Up on my hobby-horse, that's what Kelita says. She gets fed-up, hearing me talk like this."

Rachel smiled and shook her head in

reassurance. She was amazed at this revelation of Garfield's hidden self. It was true, she had suspected that he might not be the ruthless tycoon he seemed, but she had never dreamed that he could be secretly hankering after the poverty-stricken childhood of a labourer's son while he was concluding business deals worth millions. She wondered how he had achieved his present position. By hard work, almost certainly, there had been no inherited wealth to help him on his way. However he had done it, he had to be admired.

"Kelita doesn't understand, you see," he went on after a moment. "Never knew it as a kiddy, too late to learn now. I made a mistake with her, I freely admit it. Wanted her to have all we never had. Sent her to good schools, sent her abroad, got her introductions to all the right people. Well, she had it all, but there's something she never had, something that I've only really learned to value in the past year or two. Something that's nothing to do with money, but it was there in my dad's terraced house, and in my grandparent's cottage, poor as they were. Know what I mean, Rachel, or am I talking nonsense?"

"I know what you mean." Impulsively, Rachel reached out and laid her hand on his. Garfield stared down at it for a moment, looking at her slim brown palm resting on his thick fingers. When he raised his eyes, she saw that they had darkened, were even a little moist.

"Rachel," he began huskily, and she held her breath. But what he was about to say never materialised. There was the sudden bang of a door from inside the house and a moment later Kelita appeared, exotic in a white and gold sundress that reminded Rachel of one of the less inhibited of the Greek goddesses, her hair a shimmer of platinum in the sun.

"There you are, Daddy!" she exclaimed. "Didn't you hear me call? I thought you'd left the place for burglars to walk in — oh, hullo. It's Miss Grant — Rachel — isn't it? Is that your car outside? Is Lorne with you?"

"No, he sent me over on my own this time." Rachel watched the disappointment and sighed. Lorne really oughtn't to let this girl, with her brittle veneer of sophistication, fall for him; it simply wasn't fair. "Your father wanted to go over a few points about the car design with me."

Kelita nodded, losing interest, and sank into a long chair, stretching out slim golden legs. She held out her hand for a glass of lemonade. "It's so *hot!* I don't know how you can work in this heat, Rachel. It just makes me want to lie in the sun all day and soak it up." She cast a complacent eye over her tanned skin. "Of course, if you have to work for a living I suppose you just accept it. It was too hot to bear it in London, that's why I came down. I've asked a few friends along for the weekend, they should be here any time. That's all right, isn't it?"

"Well, yes, I suppose so." Garfield frowned. "But you ought to give more notice, Kelita, I've told you before. Give Mrs Appleby a chance to get rooms ready and plan the meals. I mean, someone's got to make all the beds and that's not really her job, and young Sally's gone off for the day now. How many will there be? Will they be here for dinner?"

"Oh, four or five." Kelita waved a careless hand. "And you don't need to worry about meals, we'll have a barbecue. Or go to a pub. You don't need to fuss, Daddy, these are *my* friends, not yours. They're not stuffy. They'll just take it as it comes. I'll go and see old Apple-pie now if it'll make you any happier." She got up and swayed indoors. She certainly knew how to use that delectable body of hers, Rachel thought, watching her.

"Take it as it comes," Garfield said gloomily. "I know just what that means. Barbecues in the garden, so poor Joe Appleby has to clean up every morning. Sleeping till all hours so that the rooms can't be done till nearly lunchtime, if then — but what can you do?" His indulgence returned. "They're young, and I never had the chance to do those things. Why should I deny it to them?"

He'll never learn, Rachel thought, gazing at him. He'd always react in the same way — giving in to Kelita all along the line and then wondering where he'd gone wrong. It was in his nature — that generous, loving nature that didn't show in the tough businessman side of him, but overflowed when he was in his home setting. He should have had a wife who would love him back, making the simple home life he craved. And four or five children who could share equally in his generosity, so that none of them became too spoilt.

"I'll have to go soon," she said softly. "Thank you for the delicious lunch. And tell Mrs Appleby her lemonade is marvellous. We'll be in touch about the designs."

Garfield rose to his feet and accompanied her through the house to her car.

"Thank you for coming, Rachel. It's been good, having you to talk to." He took her hand, standing close. "You'll come over again, won't you? Not on business — just so we can have a meal together and a talk. It's done me good today, I'll tell you that. I've talked to you like I haven't talked to anyone for years."

Rachel looked up into the heavy face, seeing the loneliness that lay behind it, the bewilderment that was going to increase as Kelita grew older, became more wayward. Didn't Garfield Holt have any real friends, just business acquaintances?

"I'd like that," she said, and gave him a smile. "Thank you very much."

She disengaged herself and slipped into her car. It started at once and Garfield stepped back as it slid forward. Rachel gave him a wave and the car moved smoothly down the drive.

When she reached the bend and glanced back, he was still standing there in front of his house; a solitary, lonely figure. A man who had concentrated so hard on his business, and his only daughter, that he now had nothing else. And when he had lost the one, as he was bound to do, what then? Would his interest in the other desert him as well?

And could the same thing happen to Lorne Quentin, a few years from now? Would he too be solitary, without family or any real friends, living a lonely, somehow pathetic life?

It didn't seem possible, not for a man like Lorne. And in any case, there was nothing Rachel could do about it.

Eight

"Yes, that's fine. Plenty of chairs. Not too formal, with the small tables rather more scattered than usual. Shortbread and plates on the tables, sherry handed out as people come in, with *one* refill — we mustn't forget most of them will be driving home — and the cake itself on the top table, to be cut by Arthur after the toasts and then taken round. Grape juice for the more abstemious; yes, I think that's all."

Lorne stood in the centre of the canteen, looking round at the decorations, the banner that proclaimed A Happy Retirement to Arthur, and the white-covered tables. Glasses sparkled on a side table while on the main table, set for Lorne, Rachel, Mike Dalton and a few other chief executives, plus of course Arthur himself, stood a magnificent iced cake.

"Well, you've certainly done him proud," Rachel commented, coming to stand beside Lorne. "I should think it'll be a day he'll remember for the rest of his life. Even without the ticket to Canada."

"Yes, that should really top it all." Lorne smiled at her. "It was a brilliant idea of yours, giving him that. And you're sure he has no idea?"

"None at all. And I've made absolutely sure he has no other immediate plans — he can be ready to get used to the idea, make his arrangements for his cat to be boarded, and fly in two weeks' time. And his daughter's confirmed that she's expecting him."

"You're a marvel," Lorne said, slipping his arm round her shoulders and giving her a slight squeeze. "Devious — but a marvel."

Rachel stood still in his light embrace. It was weeks since Lorne had touched her and she had almost schooled herself to forget just how his fingers could burn through her skin and set her nerves on fire. She had almost persuaded herself that he didn't affect her any more. Now she knew that it wasn't true. The flame was still there; still at white heat.

"Oh, it was easy enough," she said lightly, thankful that her voice wasn't betraying her feelings. "I just told Arthur I had friends visiting the city his daughter lives in and suggested they might like to contact her. He was quite happy to give me her address and I phoned her straightaway.

She was delighted with the whole scheme and promised not to give the slightest hint when she wrote to her father — and that was it."

"Like I said," Lorne repeated, his eyes smoky as they looked down at hers, his face suddenly intent. "Devious, but —"

There was no knowing what he'd been about to say next. Julie approached them at that moment with a list in her hand and a worried frown on her face. Lorne dropped his arm from Rachel's shoulder and turned to deal with the problem, and Rachel moved away, hoping that any observers might see nothing but casual friendliness between Lorne and herself. It seemed to come easily enough to him to give that impression, but she'd worked hard to achieve it — and it hadn't been made any easier by his attitude over Ben. In fact, if she hadn't known better she might almost have thought he was jealous!

It was now nearly a month since their confrontation over Ben's designs, and she had managed to come to terms with the fact that Lorne had turned down the Indian T. It had taken her some hard thinking before she came to the reluctant conclusion that Lorne had every right to refuse the proposition, and she'd been even more reluctant to admit that he was probably right. In a commercial sense, anyway. She still wished that they could have been the firm to produce the unconventional vehicle and play a part in opening up some of the remoter parts of the Third World. So much could be brought to them — food, medical supplies, education, better farming equipment and methods — if only the right transport could be found. And she believed as strongly as Ben did that this could be it.

Nevertheless, she had been forced to accept Lorne's ruling and continue to work with him in reasonable amity. It hadn't been quite so hard as she'd expected. She could not deny that Lorne *was* a good employer, courteous and considerate, expecting the best and giving it himself. He was stimulating, exacting and always appreciative. If only, she thought wryly, he weren't so damned *attractive*. It was almost too much to expect any woman to cope with.

She could only feel relief that he seemed to have recovered from his early attraction to her. He never gave her the assessing glance now, never let his eyes move slowly over her in the way that had never failed to melt her bones; had never touched her, even accidentally, until this afternoon. But neither did he ostentatiously avoid her. He treated her, in fact, as she'd always wanted to be treated — as a colleague, nothing more.

The fact that she longed for his touch, for a deeper smile, that she had lain awake at nights thinking of him, picturing him, was just something she had to overcome. And, until this afternoon, when he'd slipped that casual arm around her shoulders and set the whole fire burning again, she'd believed she was succeeding.

"Right, that's settled," Lorne said, joining her again. "You and Julie have done a grand job between you. The staff should be arriving any minute now." He glanced at his watch.

"And Arthur?" Rachel asked.

"He went home at lunchtime to change and I've sent a car to pick him up. He's scheduled to arrive last, when everyone's here and ready to welcome him." The door from the factory opened and people began to trickle in. The whole factory had the last hour of the afternoon off to celebrate Arthur's retirement, and many of them had brought best suits and dresses to change into. The festive atmosphere induced by the decorations and banner increased as the canteen filled with the sound of laughter. The waitresses from the executive dining-room began to circulate, offering sherry, and Lorne glanced at his watch again.

"Any moment now." He strode to the door and disappeared through it.

Rachel found Mike Dalton at her elbow. She smiled up at him. "Lorne's like a small boy having his birthday party. You'd think this had all been done for his benefit, not Arthur's!"

"Oh, he likes the chance to unbend and show his appreciation. It means a lot to him, you know, this factory and the people who work here. It's so *local* — everyone comes from villages nearby instead of some vast conurbation, they know each other and they know Lorne. Knew his father, even his grandfather. I suppose in a way old Arthur's a symbol of all that — the old way of life, when everyone worked for the Big House, linking with the new. Quentin's has bridged the gap better than most old estates, and done it in an unusual way, with industry. Yet we've never lost the rural atmosphere of the area. In a strange sort of way, it's an important part of the whole thing."

"Yes." Rachel sipped her sherry. The

door at the far end of the canteen opened and everyone turned as Lorne and Arthur came in together. The old craftsman stopped, staring at the transformation in the room where he had eaten his midday meal for the past fifty years. Slowly, he walked forward, taking in the blue and gold streamers, the banner, the neat white tables. Last of all, he looked at the cake and Rachel was near enough to see his pale blue eyes fill with tears.

"You shouldn't 'ave," he said, turning to Lorne. "You shouldn't 'ave done all this. It's — it's too much. I'm only a skilled labourer. I don't ask for this kind of thing."

"You didn't have to ask, Arthur," Lorne said, and there was a warmth in his voice that Rachel had never heard before. "I've done it because I wanted to — because, to me, you're worth it. But I'm not going to tell you all that now — it would spoil my speech." He took up a small wooden gavel and rapped it sharply to gain everyone's attention; then, standing easily by the top table and speaking with a pleasant infor-mality, he told the assembled workforce how Arthur Morris had worked all his life for Quentin's, how he'd given unswerving loyalty all those years, how he'd passed on his own high standards to all those he'd helped to train. "He's more than an employee to me," Lorne finished. "He's a friend. And that's the way I want it to be with all of you. That's the way we work here at Quentin Motors and Arthur Morris is our prime example." He raised his glass. "I have great pleasure now in proposing a toast. To Arthur Morris — a long and happy retirement!"

The toast was echoed with enthusiasm, and then Lorne turned to draw Arthur forward. "I know you're going to be asked to make a speech in a moment," he said with a smile, "but before you start on one of those *interminable* stories of the old days —" everyone, including Arthur, laughed "— I want to give you this. Not a gold watch — you've always been an impeccable timekeeper. Not a set of spare parts for you to spend your time assembling your own car. Not even a jigsaw puzzle to while away those long hours of retirement. No, we've thought long and hard, and we think these two things are what you'll appreciate most. A small replica of the first car Quentin's ever put on the road." He handed over an exquisite little model that made Rachel gasp with delight. "And this. A return ticket to Canada, to visit your daughter who's airing your bed at this very minute and expecting you on Tuesday week."

He stepped back slightly, leaving Arthur staring in amazed delight at the two gifts. The watching workers cheered loudly and began to call for a speech. Arthur looked at them; looked at Lorne; looked back at the presents. He opened his mouth, but there was no sound.

"All right, Arthur," Lorne said, smiling broadly. "Take your time."

"First time old Arthur's ever been lost for words!" someone called out from the floor, and there was a general laugh.

Arthur shook his head slowly. His mouth was working and Rachel, smiling as broadly as all the rest, felt a sudden stab of alarm. Wasn't there something just a little odd about the old man's reactions, the twist of his face? She stepped forward, and at the same moment Lorne caught at Arthur's arm, concern creasing his brow. Arthur tried to speak again; failed; and the whole audience, silenced now, gave a gasp as he sagged between Lorne and Rachel, his knees giving way completely as they caught him in their arms and lowered him to a chair.

There was an immediate outbreak of chatter, but Rachel wasn't listening. Her whole concern was with Arthur, clearly unconscious now, his face a greyish pallor. Anxiously, she looked up at Lorne and he caught her glance.

"We'd better get a doctor. Mike, help me carry him through to my apartment. Then come back here and carry on with the party. Make as little of it as you can, say he's just a bit overcome and lying down for a few minutes. Julie, get the waitresses to go round with the sherry. Get the cake cut and take it round too. Rachel, come with me, will you?"

Rachel preceded Mike and Lorne out through the door and along the corridor to Lorne's quarters. Obeying Lorne's instructions, she opened the big oak door to let them through with their burden, then closed it behind her and followed them into a spacious living-room, enlarged by a hexagonal glass sun-room filled with plants. Lorne and Mike carried Arthur to a large sofa and laid him down.

"We ought to loosen his clothing," Lorne said, staring down anxiously at the old man. "Rachel, d'you know anything about first aid?"

"A little." She came over, noticing how much smaller Arthur looked now, and how frail. He should never have been allowed to work so long, she thought, but knew he had refused to retire until forced to. "Yes, loosen his collar and tie." She took up his wrist. "His pulse isn't too bad — a bit weak. I think we ought to phone for an ambulance, though."

"Mike's gone to do that." Lorne glanced up as the door opened and his face cleared as the factory nurse came in. "Oh, Sister, thank goodness you've come. I was about to send for you. Miss Grant was just loosening his clothing, is there anything else we ought to be doing?"

"There's not a great deal, I'm afraid." The nurse frowned down at the patient and, like Rachel, took his wrist. "It could be just a faint or it could be a heart attack, or a stroke. Has he been complaining at all, do you know — pains in his chest or arms, any odd feelings?" They both shook their heads helplessly. "Well, his workmates might know. Has an ambulance been called?"

"It's on its way." Mike came back from the phone and joined the anxious circle round Arthur. "There's nothing else we can do?"

"You might as well get back to the canteen," Lorne said. "Don't let anyone get worried, but don't encourage them to hang about either. Tell them he'll be back to make his speech in a few days — and let's just hope he's fit to." His face was drawn with anxiety, Rachel noticed. He really cared about Arthur. In fact, he was a caring man generally. A man of deep sensitivity; deep feelings.

And as she watched him, bending over an old man whom he had known all his life, a man who had worked loyally for three generations of Quentins, Rachel felt a window open in her mind. It was a window she had kept fastened in spite of all the attempts of her instincts to thrust it wide. It let in a knowledge that she felt must always have been there; that she just hadn't wanted to face.

It wasn't an infatuation she'd felt for Lorne Quentin. It wasn't just the reaction of a woman who'd kept physical attraction at bay for too long. It was more — much, much more than that.

It was love that she felt. A deep, strong and abiding love. A love that encompassed all her physical desires and blended them with an emotional, a spiritual longing to share her life with this man. A love that had, almost without her knowing it, put its roots deep down into her soul and could never be shaken loose.

"Well, there he goes," Lorne said, turning back into the house. "Let's hope he'll be all right."

Arthur had been taken to the hospital, the factory nurse going with him in the ambulance. He had begun to recover consciousness as they had lifted him on to the stretcher, but his eyelids had barely flickered before he had slipped back into sleep. Whether it was a good sign or not, Rachel had no idea.

Lorne passed a hand across his brow. "I'd better go back to the canteen, soothe them with a few words," he said wearily. "Not that I feel like soothing anyone — I want someone to soothe me! But I can't just let the party dwindle away."

Rachel watched him, feeling an almost overwhelming desire to take that dark head on her breast, smooth the hair back from a forehead that was pale now, touch the chiselled lips with hers in comfort . . . "Why don't you come straight back here?" she suggested before she could change her mind. "I'll have a pot of tea ready for you, if that's what you'd like — or maybe you feel like something stronger."

"Tea," said Lorne, "would be ideal. It's supposed to be good for shock, isn't it?"

He smiled at her, his features lightened momentarily with gratitude. "Bless you, Rachel, that would be wonderful. Provided you stay and share the tea with me."

He disappeared, and Rachel found her way to his kitchen and put on the kettle. In spite of her worry about Arthur, she couldn't help looking around with interest. This was Lorne's home, the place where he was most himself — what could it tell her about him?

The kitchen was big and just cluttered enough to be comfortable — and the clutter was mostly deliberate; no piles of old newspapers or opened tins, but earthenware pots crammed with flourishing plants, a few interesting posters on the walls, a cluster of cooking implements hanging from the ceiling. A large Aga took up most of one wall, and in the centre of the kitchen was a long table with a scrubbed wooden top. In one corner was a basket with a huge orange cat curled up in it.

Rachel found tea, milk and sugar and set them on a tray together with two bone china cups which she took from the Welsh dresser. The kettle boiled and she made the tea, then carried it through to the sitting-room.

To her surprise, Lorne was already there. He was standing by the open patio doors of the sun-room, gazing out into the garden. He turned as Rachel came through and cleared a glass-topped cane table for the tray.

"Thanks, Rachel. That's good of you." He gave her the choice of seats and she chose a swinging bamboo chair. "I'm sorry, that was all rather a shock for me. For us all."

"But mostly for you," Rachel said gently. She'd realised a lot of things during the past half-hour. "Arthur meant a lot to you, didn't he?"

"Yes, he did." Lorne sipped his tea and closed his eyes. "He was — well, he was almost the most important figure in my childhood. Sounds odd, that, doesn't it? I had both parents living. But they were remote from me. My father in the way that a lot of fathers used to be remote from their children, because of the hours they worked — nothing unusual in that. But my mother — well, I never saw much of her. I may have told you, I spent most of my school holidays with other children. That was because she quite simply didn't want me here."

"Didn't *want* you? But —"

"It's quite true. She never did want children — had me because of the family name, was hugely relieved that I was a son and she needn't bother with any more, and then went her own sweet way. I had a very good nanny, fortunately, until I was seven; then she was taken ill — she was past retirement age and had only stayed on to be with me until I went to prep-school. It was Arthur's wife who was called in to look after me then. She'd worked in the nursery of one of my mother's friends as an assistant. She stayed until I went to prep-school, and then came in during the holidays." He paused. "I saw a lot of Arthur in those days. Meg — that was his wife — used to take me down to their cottage and I'd spend the day there with her, helping to bake cakes or weed the garden. And at the weekends, Arthur was there too. They were more like family to me than my own." He shook his head. "And Edna, their daughter, the one in Canada — I didn't realise until you mentioned her that she'd even left the country. It shook me to see just how little I've known about Arthur since Meg died. And now . . ." His words drifted away.

"I'm sure he understood," Rachel said gently. "He never felt you'd let him down."

"Let him down," Lorne repeated. "You used those words once before. About children and their parents. You said the only way children could really let their parents down was by not loving them." He was silent for a moment and Rachel wondered if he was thinking of the mother who hadn't loved him, and had let him down. But he went on: "We were talking about Kelita. Can you wonder now that I feel sorry for her, losing her mother when she was seven?"

"But that isn't the same," Rachel said, following her own train of thought. "Kelita's mother didn't stop loving her, she died. And she's the apple of Garfield's eye."

"It was the way she spent her childhood I was thinking of, not the reasons for it," Lorne said, and Rachel wondered whether she had offended him by implying that his own mother hadn't loved him. But wasn't that what he'd said himself? "Alone with a succession of nannies and then boarding-school, hardly seeing her father, even if he did think the world of her. What chance does a child have of growing up normally?"

"I honestly don't know. I had such a different childhood myself, so secure, almost too sheltered. But, in the end, aren't we all responsible for ourselves? I mean — you've grown up, overcome your unhappy start. Don't we all at some time have to stop blaming our parents or other early influences and be answerable for our own behaviour? None of us has the right to expect our parents to be perfect — we'd all be terrified to have children at all if that were so."

Lorne opened his eyes and looked at her for a long moment, his expression unreadable. Then he nodded slightly. "You're probably right. We all have to overcome our Peter Pan complexes and become adult in the end. It just takes some of us a little longer, that's all. And a few of us never quite manage it . . ." He sat up abruptly. "Is there any more tea?"

Rachel got up and took his cup. He really did look exhausted, she thought compassionately, as if the events of the afternoon had been a kind of watershed, breaking that seemingly endless dynamic drive of his and leaving him floundering. He was lying back in the long chair, eyes closed again, face ashen. On a sudden impulse, she bent and with tender fingertips smoothed back a lock of dark hair.

Lorne's eyes opened. They were the dark, soft grey of doves' wings and they were very close to hers. She could feel his breath on her cheek.

She stayed perfectly still, bending over him, her fingers still touching his hair. Neither of them moved; their eyes searched each other, slowly, wonderingly. Then, as if dragged by an invisible cord, Lorne's hand reached up to touch her cheek. Slowly, his fingers trailed down the smooth column of her neck, shaped her shoulder, slid round to her back; and then drew her down to him.

"Rachel," he muttered huskily as his lips touched hers. And then, catching her against him so suddenly that she lost balance and fell into his arms: "Oh, *God* . . . Rachel, my love . . ."

Rachel lay in his arms, totally unable to resist the onslaught of hungry kisses with which Lorne was almost consuming her; unable at first even to respond as his lips rained a torrent of soft yet demanding caresses over her face, her throat, her eyelids, her ears. She could feel his fingers, tense with longing as he ran them through her silky hair, trembling as they slid down her neck and bit gently into her shoulders under the smooth, fine cotton of her blouse. The restraint he was clearly exercising came more, she dimly recognised, from a fear of letting himself go than from any consideration for her. Not that he wouldn't be a considerate lover — the tenderness of his touch told her that he would be. But there was a passion in him, a deep, driving urgency, that he was holding back, and she guessed that this was something he always did hold back. Something vital to his personality, a part of himself that was kept locked away.

He'll never be able to love properly while he's still locked up inside, she thought suddenly. And that's why he's never married, why he's always so careful to keep his relationships light. He's afraid . . .

She had a sudden longing to be the one to unlock his frozen heart, the one with the key that would set him free. Dimly, she knew that it would take more than a few kisses, that he needed care and sensitivity, but even as she acknowledged this, her own reeling senses were taking over, driving all sense from her mind, his touch sending her dizzy with desire. She wanted only to love and be loved by him. For the first time in years, her own sensual needs were paramount, and she knew that she was about to step over the brink and yield to the demands of her own body.

For a few minutes, all thought was suspended as their desire swept them along. And then Lorne lifted her away from him and stood up. For a moment, unable to bear the thought of parting even for a few seconds, they stood close together, bodies moulding; then Lorne lifted her against him and as she curled her legs around his waist he carried her into the room and laid her on the sofa where only an hour ago old Arthur had lain unconscious. The memory returned to them both simultaneously. Rachel saw Lorne's hesitation as he lowered himself beside her, saw his eyes darken, and turned her head aside.

"The hospital," she murmured. "They said they'd ring . . . Lorne, we can't — not until we know."

"Oh, God," he muttered. "For a moment, I'd forgotten. I'd forgotten everything — everything except you, my love."

Rachel searched his face. Could she make him forget again? Could she, with a few movements, a few caresses, bring him back to that exquisite state of delirious rapture which they'd shared until only a few seconds ago? With her new knowledge of him, of herself, she believed that she could. But she would not make that first move. It would be ecstasy to do so, but afterwards, wouldn't Lorne blame her for making him desert his childhood friend, the man who had been like a father to him? He had called her his love; wouldn't he love her more for letting go now, for bringing him gently back to earth? Wasn't there every possibility that this scene could be continued later, when Arthur's situation was resolved — one way or the other?

Drugged with desire, Rachel found it hard to answer yes to all those questions, to relinquish what had so nearly been hers. But with an effort for which she was later grateful, she raised herself on the couch and pushed him gently away.

"Go and ring the hospital now," she said softly. "Ask them how he is. They've had time to examine him — they may be able to tell you something."

"Yes." His eyes were still on hers, hazy, clouded, dark. He moved like a man in a trance as he lifted himself away from her, his hands reluctant to let her go. He went slowly from the room to the telephone.

Rachel stayed on the couch for a few moments and then, recovering herself, she stood up. She wandered about, dazed, drinking in the fact that she was here, in Lorne's own room, amongst furniture he knew and loved. That these were his pictures, his books, that in this rack of records was the music he loved — the music they both loved. Idly, she picked out a symphony — Rimsky-Korsakov's *Sheherezade*, the music of a love story as tempestuous as the stormy sea — and placed it on the turntable. When Lorne returned, she would put it on, and then . . .

A sheet of paper on a nearby table caught her eye. She turned and looked at it properly, recognising the design for a car. So Lorne was a workaholic, bringing his designs here to work on in the evenings. The busy socialite of the gossip columns? Her lips curved in a smile. Apart from a dinner or two, the odd business lunch, Lorne seemed never to stop working. Well, maybe that was all about to change.

What *was* this design he was working on, anyway? She bent to look closer and froze.

Ben's design for the Indian T stared up at her. It had been changed, modified, improved in what she recognised as Lorne's hand. But it was definitely Ben's — the design Lorne had turned down out of hand, refused to have anything to do with.

The design she'd carelessly left in his office for a whole day, giving him plenty of time to copy it before she'd collected it later that afternoon.

A sound from outside told her that Lorne had finished talking on the phone and was about to come back. Her heart pounded as she rolled up the drawings and ran across the room. She was halfway through the door to the sun-room when Lorne appeared from the hall.

"I spoke to the Sister," he said, his voice exhausted. "She said they haven't finished their tests yet but Arthur seems to have suffered a slight stroke. It doesn't appear to be serious and he should recover quite quickly and have no ill-effects. They're pretty sure he's going to be all right."

Rachel stood in the doorway, the drawings concealed behind her skirt. Part of her longed to run to him, to take him in her arms, rejoice with him and comfort him. But another part — and it was a much greater part — was hating him for what he'd been about to do to Ben. For stealing a design he'd scorned, a design that hadn't been intended for profit. And for implicating her too — for wouldn't Ben think that she had a part in it, that she'd known Lorne was copying his plans, that she too was mercenary enough, unscrupulous enough to filch the work of someone who'd thought of her as his friend . . .

She stood quite still, staring at Lorne, a

more furious rage than she had ever known before simmering inside her. The strength of her feelings frightened her. It was as if they could be relieved only by violence, but a violence that wouldn't, this time, stop at merely throwing things. She wanted to strike out at Lorne for his betrayal, to scream her hatred into his face; to rip her nails down the skin she'd been kissing only minutes ago, strip away all pretence, all hypocrisy from the man she had been foolish enough to love.

"Rachel?" Lorne was watching her, a puzzled frown on his face. "Rachel, is anything the matter?"

"That's marvellous news," she said quickly, her voice brittle with despair. "I'm so glad. You'll be wanting to go and see Arthur, I'm sure. Give him my love, won't you, and tell him to get well soon. And you'd better let his daughter know, or shall I do that?" She backed away as she spoke, her heart hammering against her ribs as she watched him approach her. He mustn't come near her — mustn't see that she had Ben's drawings — mustn't touch her. If he touched her, those last frail shreds of control would disappear.

Ever since that scene with Graham, when he had told her he was leaving her

260

for Sue, Rachel had feared her own temper. She had been shocked that night by her eruption into near-violence. Throwing things, even pillows or books, might have been the subject of hundreds of jokes over the years, but when it happened, she had found that it left you with a feeling of guilt that was hard to get rid of. It had been no use telling herself she'd been provoked, that his behaviour had driven her to it, that no one would have blamed her.

The memory of the clock, hitting him on the shoulder, the thought of the table lamp she'd unplugged, even though she'd never actually thrown it, had appalled her. I could have hurt him, she thought, really hurt him. And she'd understood, and been horrified by the understanding, just how easy it could be to do real damage to a fellow human being.

Since then, Rachel had striven to learn to control the temper she had feared so much. She had read books, gone through a number of mental exercises, even taken counselling, and until now she'd believed that she had gained full control over her anger. She no longer swallowed it, but allowed herself to express it as and when it arose, and on the whole her reasons had

261

been acceptable, and the points she made acknowledged by others. Her anger had never been allowed to simmer and ferment, with the danger of explosion never far away.

"I'll have to go now," she said rapidly, "I'd forgotten I had to get home early today. Sorry to rush away, Lorne — do let me know if there's anything I can do, won't you? And don't forget to give Arthur my love. Tell him I'll come in and see him myself as soon as he's allowed visitors."

She was at the sun-room door now, ready to escape across the lawns to the car park. Her bag was somewhere, but she couldn't wait to pick it up — she had the keys to the cottage in her car, so it wasn't essential. Her only thought now was to get away, to get away from Lorne before she cracked entirely. And she needed to sort out her tangled emotions, to know whether it was love she felt for this man, or hatred.

Feeling Ben's drawings in her hand and knowing just what they'd meant to him, there didn't seem to be much doubt that it was hatred.

Nine

Rachel did not see Lorne again for several days. She was aware that he had tried to contact her; on that first evening, when she'd returned to the cottage shaking with reaction, her telephone had rung half a dozen times. She had steadfastly ignored it until, afraid that Lorne would come to see why she wasn't answering, she had packed a case and fled to Exmoor for the weekend. Her parents had welcomed her without surprise, accustomed to the comings and goings of their offspring, but on the Sunday afternoon, while helping her mother in the garden, Rachel had finally broken her reserve and told the whole story, leaving out the kisses she and Lorne had shared, and the way she'd so nearly surrendered on the Friday afternoon.

"And you really believe he intends to produce Ben's designs as his own?" Mrs Grant asked. "I find that difficult to believe. He'd never get away with it, surely — isn't there any kind of copyright on these things, like on books and music? And

263

you say there's no profit in the car anyway, so what would be the point?"

"Heaven knows." Rachel shrugged. "I told you, Mum, he's a devious man. I don't think anyone really knows how his mind works. He can be charm itself when he wants to be, but underneath he's just steel, I'm sure of it. And stone. He doesn't really care about anyone but himself." She pushed away the thought of Lorne's distress over Arthur. All right, she'd believed it was genuine, but she didn't know what to believe any more.

Mrs Grant shook her head. "Well, I don't know what to say, dear. I suppose you'll have to work it out for yourself. I agree, he must have had *some* reason for having Ben's drawings copied, and it certainly seems odd in the face of his refusal to consider them. I suppose you'll give the copies to Ben? Well, after that, I suggest you leave it to him to deal with. It really isn't your business and you do work for Lorne. It might have been better if you'd faced him with it there and then."

Rachel had come to this uncomfortable conclusion herself, and she couldn't really tell her mother just why she hadn't, why she'd been in such turmoil when she found the drawings. She shrugged and muttered something non-committal, wanting now to get off the subject. Her mother gave her a keen glance.

"I think this bed is clear now," she observed, rising from her kneeling-pad. "Those buttercups really have to be weeded out at the first signs or they take over completely. Thank you for helping, Rachel. Let's go in and make some tea, shall we?"

Rachel returned to Herefordshire feeling calmer, but still not looking forward to seeing Lorne. Fortunately, she knew, he'd been due to go away on Monday, to attend a meeting in Munich. That would take up most of his week. Perhaps by the time they met they would both be back to their normal cool relationship.

If only she hadn't fallen in love with him, she thought miserably. It was so much easier to hate a man you already disliked. But when someone you loved did something that was, well, no less than a betrayal, it hurt badly. She remembered Graham, and her feelings when he had married Sue. That had been painful enough, but beside this it had been nothing.

She'd been right to tell herself not to get involved with Lorne Quentin. She'd known from the very beginning that it could only mean heartbreak. So why — *why* — had she let it happen?

There was no word from Lorne, no message at the cottage and no more telephone calls. When Rachel went in to work on Monday, there was nothing apart from the normal requests to deal with various projects. The latest news from the hospital, Julie told her, was that Arthur was doing well and expected to leave in a few days. He wouldn't be able to fly to Canada next week as planned, but there seemed to be no reason why he shouldn't go the week after. He was looking forward to seeing her if she had time to visit him.

"Of course I've got time," Rachel said. "I'll go this evening. And I'll be going over to see Garfield Holt tomorrow, so I won't be in until Wednesday." She'd have to decide what to do about Ben's drawings by then, she thought unhappily. They had become a burden, lying heavily on her mind. Almost, she wished she hadn't found them, hadn't known anything about them. Then, when Lorne had come back from the phone on Friday she would have been waiting him, still soft with love, ready to go on from where they'd left off and — oh, *hell!*

And how would you have felt after *that*, when you'd found out about Ben's plans? she asked herself sardonically, knowing that she must eventually have discovered Lorne's duplicity. A whole lot worse, that's how.

She was thankful to be going over to the Cotswolds next day, leaving Quentin Court with all its painful reminders behind for a few hours. This time, the sun wasn't shining; the morning was grey, with a faint mist hanging over the meadows and a slight chill in the air. Rachel hesitated over her dress, then decided she knew Garfield well enough now to put on a pair of slim white jeans. Knowing it might clear later and turn hot again, she wore a loose, sleeveless T-shirt over them, its turquoise pattern contrasting with her flame-coloured hair to give a kingfisher effect that seldom failed to cheer her up. Over the T-shirt, she slipped a white, loose-knit sweater.

She still hadn't decided what to do about Ben's plans, and was beginning to wish she'd confronted Lorne with them on Friday afternoon. But the shock — coming after Arthur's collapse and her own near-surrender — had thrown her completely.

All she'd wanted to do was to get away, to clear her mind, to think. Not that *thinking* had helped much, she reflected grimly. She still wasn't any nearer to a solution, and Lorne must by now have realised the designs were missing. He wouldn't have much difficulty in deducing who had taken them. So why hadn't he contacted her, demanded their return?

It could only be because he realised that she knew what his possession of the drawings meant; because he too was afraid of a confrontation. Or maybe he was so arrogantly sure of himself that he didn't care? Thought she was so besotted, she wouldn't lift a finger to stop his monstrous plans?

If only there were something she could do to help Ben. If only she could find someone else to back him.

The sun had begun to break through the cloud when Rachel turned up the drive of Garfield's house, but the sky was still predominantly grey and she was glad of the hot coffee he offered her when she arrived. He led her into the sitting-room, where it was ready on a low table, and Rachel sank gratefully into one of the big armchairs.

"I've been looking forward to seeing you again, Rachel," Garfield said, offering her a plate of Mrs Appleby's homemade biscuits.

"These little conferences are beginning to make quite a bright spot in my life. It's good of you to come all this way."

"Oh, I dare say it'll all go on the bill!" Rachel answered lightly. "But I must admit I enjoy it too. It's such a lovely drive over, and so peaceful here — I can hardly believe you're such a busy tycoon, you seem to have all the time in the world."

"Only when you're here, I'm afraid. I spend a good deal of my time in London, as you know, and even here I keep in touch by fax and modem. And I have two secretaries here as well — they have their own offices in the house. Oh yes, it's quite a hive of industry here, in spite of appearances!"

"I see." Rachel looked round at the comfortable room. There was no hint of the chatter of typewriters, the bleeping of computers that must be going on quite nearby. "Well, perhaps we'd better add our quota to all this hard work." She got to her feet and gave Garfield a smile, waiting for him to lead her through to the study.

For a minute, he didn't move. He looked at her as if he wanted to say something — something he found difficult. Rachel felt a queer moment of unease and caught her breath; then it was past and Garfield was smiling with his usual geniality and turning towards the door, already talking about the car designs.

It must have been imagination, she thought as she followed him. What could Garfield have to say to her that he found difficult?

Their discussions took Rachel's mind off her problems for a while, and Garfield too seemed to relax as they absorbed themselves in the designs. Almost all the points had been agreed now, and he looked pleased as they went back to the small dining-room — the breakfast-room, Garfield called it — for lunch. "I like this better," he explained, taking Rachel into the light, prettily-furnished room. "The main dining-room's fine for a big party, but I feel a bit lost in there on my own." His secretaries were evidently eating somewhere else. Rachel had met them this morning, a competent-looking middle-aged woman and a young, rather fluffy blonde.

"Is Kelita away?" she enquired, unfolding her napkin and accepting a glass of wine.

"No, she's at home this week. Just out to lunch with some friend or other." A look of pride crossed his face. "I probably shouldn't be saying this, but, well, I've got hopes that Kelita will be settling down soon. There's a man in the offing, I'm sure of it, and I think I know who it is." He gave Rachel a meaning look. "I'd better not say any more, perhaps. Though *you* might be able to make a good guess."

Rachel felt cold. Did he mean Lorne? She thought of Kelita's open flirtation with him on their first visit here, her invitation to the cocktail party. She remembered the day Ben had come to Quentin's, when they'd seen Kelita with Lorne in the car park, going to lunch. And no doubt there'd been other meetings, meetings Garfield knew about. Meetings here. Dinners. Moonlight bathes in that rose-scented swimming pool.

"It'd be a good match for Kelita," Garfield was saying. "Lorne's quite a bit older than she is, of course, but that's not a bad thing. She needs an older man, to keep her in order. Better than some of the other young fools she runs around with. There was one in particular — Rupert, he was called, did you ever hear such a name? — I was quite worried about him for a time. One of those chinless wonders, you know? I'd have put my foot down if that had gone on, I can tell you. Plenty of money and never done a day's work in his life." He shook his head. "That's the trouble with all Kelita's set, of course. None of them know how to work. Honest toil, that's the thing." He gave Rachel a quick glance. "Don't you agree?"

"Yes, I think I do." Rachel helped herself to salad to go with the delicious lasagne that Mrs Appleby had brought in. "Work you can enjoy and feel is worthwhile is the most important thing in life. Well, almost."

"Almost, yes." The heavy face settled into sad lines for a moment. "But it isn't everything, is it? I'm not saying that. There's still — well, family life if you like. That's important, too." He hesitated and then added: "That's what I've missed, in a way, in spite of having Kelita. And, well, tell me if I'm talking out of turn, Rachel, but I get the feeling you miss it too."

Rachel dropped her fork. She shook her head. "No, no, you're wrong, Garfield. I come from a big family — four of us — and we're all still quite close, I was down with my parents only this weekend —"

"That's not what I meant," he said. "I meant our *own* family life. A wife, a husband, children. We're both rather lonely people, Rachel. I know I am, anyway. And I think, if you're honest . . . ?"

272

Rachel felt her mind twist in confusion. Already she had realised that Garfield was more perceptive than she had first thought. But this was unexpected.

She couldn't lie to him, though; not when he was letting her see his own frailties.

"Yes," she said quietly, "you're right. I *do* get lonely. I — I was let down once, you see and, well, I haven't been keen to repeat the experience."

Garfield nodded. "And I haven't remarried because I never found anyone I could bear to put in the place of my Jeanie." A tiny pause. "Until now." He looked at her again, a look so full of hope and longing and entreaty that Rachel felt the tears come to her eyes.

"Garfield . . ." she said helplessly, holding out her hands, palms upwards.

He took one in both of his, covering her cool fingers with his warmth. "I know I'm not the kind of man you could have," he said. "I mean, you could take your pick. You're that kind of woman. But I can offer you a good home, a comfortable life, everything you could ask for. And . . . his voice dropped, and Rachel knew instinctively that his next words were ones he had only spoken to the wife he had mourned for so many years. "I could offer you love. Nothing special, mind. Just honest, simple love."

The tears were almost overflowing. Rachel gazed at him, then looked down at their clasped hands. For a moment, she allowed herself to imagine life with Garfield. Yes, he would offer her love, she knew that. He was, essentially, a simple and honest man. He would give her everything that was in his power to give — luxury homes, holidays abroad, jewels, clothes — all that. And if she wanted only to stay here, in the house she'd loved ever since she'd first set eyes on it, then he would give her that too. The life of a countrywoman, making herself a part of the community, making friends, bringing up a family . . .

Rachel blinked rapidly. If anything could tempt her, it would be that last picture, but she knew that she could never accept. Because there was nothing she could give Garfield in return. Because she could never give him the love that he'd offered her so generously.

"It isn't any good, is it?" Garfield said quietly.

"Garfield, I — I don't know what to say. I never dreamed . . ." But she'd known he admired her. She could have foreseen this, forestalled it, only she'd been too absorbed in her own feelings. She hadn't taken the time to see what was happening in Garfield's heart.

"It's all right. I didn't really dare to hope." He shrugged. "You couldn't waste yourself on an old buffer like me, I knew that really. But, well, you don't blame me for trying, do you? I had to try — to make sure." His small eyes were anxious. "I hope I haven't offended you."

"Offended me? Why should I feel offended, for heaven's sake?" Rachel gave him a tremulous smile. "I'm honoured, Garfield — honestly. I know how you felt about your wife, about marrying again. I'm very touched that you could think of putting me in her place. I only wish . . . but there it is. It wouldn't be fair to *you*, Garfield. I know you could give me so much — but I couldn't give you anything."

"You don't think there's a chance you'd ever come to love me? Just a little?" he asked wistfully, and she shook her head.

"It's not because of you, Garfield," she told him, and decided that he deserved the truth. It was the least she could give him. "It's . . . I'm in love with someone else. Oh, there's no chance it will ever come to anything, he doesn't care about me at all." The words were like a knife driving into her own heart. "But I couldn't marry you — or anyone else — feeling like this."

"I see." Garfield was looking steadily at her and she wondered in sudden panic whether he would realise it was Lorne she loved. That was the last thing she wanted when only a few minutes earlier he'd been talking about his own hopes regarding Lorne and Kelita. But a second's thought told her it was unlikely. He'd only seen her with Lorne once, and Kelita had claimed most of the attention on that occasion.

"So that's that." Garfield looked at her hand, still clasped in his, and gave it back to her with a wry smile. "I hope I haven't embarrassed you, Rachel. That's why I didn't say anything earlier — I thought if you were going to say no, and I was pretty sure you would — it was better after we'd talked business, not before. You'll be wanting to go now, I've no doubt."

"Only if you want me to. I'd still like to think we were friends, Garfield. And besides," she cast around for something that would lighten the moment, "I haven't had coffee yet!"

Garfield grinned. "No more you have! I'll call Mrs Appleby straightway." He touched the bell. "And, Rachel, about us being friends. I'd like that too. We'll make a bargain, shall we? Friends — good friends. And if there's anything you'd ever like — any help you need, anything at all — well, you'll know just where to come, won't you? I mean it, Rachel. Anything." He turned as the housekeeper came into the room with the coffee-pot. "Ah, Mrs Appleby, just what we need. And the lunch was delicious; thank you."

He really was a nice man, Rachel thought, watching him. He never failed to thank his staff for what they did, to show appreciation. And it was clear that they — the ones Rachel had met anyway — thought the world of him.

Maybe he wasn't such a lonely man after all. Maybe more people loved him than he had any idea.

They talked of other things while drinking their coffee, and the inevitable tension decreased. Rachel was relieved to find that she was quickly able to regain her more casual footing with Garfield, though she was conscious now of a new intimacy between them, as if they had travelled quite a long way during the past hour or so. He really meant it about being friends, she thought warmly, and was surprised to find how much that meant to her.

"Well, I really must be going," she declared at last, getting up. "I want to finish tidying up the plans today so they're ready for Lorne to see when he comes back." She glanced round as the door opened, and saw Kelita standing there, slender as a wand in a watery-green silk dress, her eyes almost unnaturally bright. "Hello, Kelita. How are you?"

"Very well, thank you," the girl answered politely, but there was a feverish undercurrent in her voice as she glanced quickly at her father. "Daddy, I want to go away for a few days. Just until the weekend. That's all right, isn't it?"

"Well, yes, I suppose so. You don't usually consult me about your comings and goings." He gave her a speculative look. "Going with some friends, are you?"

"Yes, yes, that's right, with some friends." Kelita spoke rapidly, flicking quick, bright little glances from Garfield to Rachel. "Just a few days away. It's rather on the spur of the moment — I'll have to go and pack straightway." She turned to go, then whipped back, her eyes glittering with excitement. "Rachel, are you in a hurry? Would you come up to my room with me — I've got something to show you."

Rachel gave Garfield a bewildered shrug, then followed the younger girl from the room. What on earth could Kelita have to show her? She'd never got the impression that the girl even liked her. And why all the excitement over a few days' holiday, when all Kelita's life was holiday anyway?

She had never been to Kelita's room before, and couldn't help stopping in delight as she entered the pretty suite, furnished in white and pale green, with sprigged curtains billowing at the open windows. The sky had cleared completely now and the sun streamed in, filling the room with light and warmth. Clothes were strewn on the bed and chairs — light summer dresses, billowing skirts, lacy blouses, silk underwear. And, Rachel saw, some particularly diaphanous nightdresses.

"Oh, I'm so *excited!*" Kelita caught at Rachel's arms and whirled her about the room, laughing. "I'm sorry, Rachel — I just *had* to tell someone, and I couldn't possibly mention it to Daddy just yet — I'm *engaged!* Isn't it wonderful? Look!"

Stunned, Rachel stared at the tiny box Kelita had produced. The lid flicked open and she caught her breath. Even Kelita's expression was subdued for a moment as they stared together at the ring that lay inside on its velvet pad. Then she was laughing again, slipping it on to her finger, holding it this way and that to catch the light.

"Isn't it beautiful?" she said in an awed voice.

"It's lovely." And, thought Rachel, extremely valuable if that huge blue stone is a real sapphire. But of course, it must be. Lorne would never give his fiancée anything less than genuine stones. "It's beautiful." Her lips were stiff as she added formally: "I hope you'll be very happy, Kelita."

"Oh, I shall, I shall," Kelita answered joyously, whisking away to dance around the room again. All her former hostility towards Rachel seemed to have disappeared. But then, she could afford to be magnanimous, couldn't she? She was engaged to Lorne. She had triumphed. "Everything's marvellous. *He's* marvellous — you don't know how marvellous, Rachel. Being *engaged* is marvellous." She laughed again and came to rest by the windowsill, leaning out so that the sunshine caught her shimmering hair. "Do you know, I thought for a while he didn't even *like* me. And then — oh, I can't explain. We just knew. Both of us. It's as if

I'd never been alive before, as if — as if I'd only just been born."

Rachel nodded. She knew the feeling — knew it only too well. In her case, it was associated with the pain of betrayal — first Graham's, now Lorne's. He must have known, even while he was kissing her last Friday afternoon, even as he prepared to make love to her. He must have known he was going to ask Kelita to marry him. Maybe he'd even bought that ring, that fabulous sapphire. He could even have had it in his pocket.

Feeling sick, she smiled and nodded at Kelita as mechanically as a doll. If nothing else, she told herself, she could hang on to what tattered shreds of pride she had left. She didn't have to let Kelita know how she felt.

"It's wonderful," she said. "And I suppose you're going off with him now." But Lorne was in Munich, wasn't he? A wild hope seized her. Could she possibly be wrong — could Kelita's lover be some other man? Could that silk underwear, those sheer nighties, be meant for someone else's delectation?

Her hope lasted no more than a few seconds. Kelita had swooped on the clothes scattered about and was folding them hastily into a leather suitcase. She nodded her answer to Rachel's question.

"Yes, that's right. I'm flying from Birmingham in three hours' time. So you can see why I couldn't tell Daddy. He'd hit the roof if he knew!" She giggled, finger to her lips. "You won't tell him, will you, Rachel? I can trust you?"

"Oh yes," Rachel said wearily, "you can trust me." She didn't bother to tell Kelita that her secrecy was needless, that Garfield would be delighted to hear his daughter was engaged to Lorne Quentin. He would probably be less delighted that she was off to spend a weekend with him in Munich, a weekend during which Rachel had no doubt they intended to spend the nights as well as the days together. No woman packed nightclothes like that simply for her own benefit.

"That's marvellous. And now I'll have to rush or I'll *never* make it." Kelita slammed the case shut and gave Rachel a quick, unexpected kiss on the cheek. "Thanks for letting me tell you, Rachel — I'll invite you to my engagement party. That's if Daddy lets me have one!" She chuckled mischievously. "Poor darling — he'll have a *fit* when he knows!" And then she was gone, flitting down the stairs with her case

282

bumping on every step, a delighted radiance shining from her like an aura, lighting up the dim passageway.

And in an odd kind of way, as Rachel stared after her and waited for pain to replace the numbness in her heart, she found herself actually liking the younger girl. All Kelita's affectations, all her pretensions had disappeared. She was just like any other excited teenager in love for the first time, seeing all her bright hopes about to come true.

Rachel went slowly down the stairs. She could remember feeling like that herself. She hoped that Kelita, who was after all an attractive youngster under her veneer of sophistication, was not going to be hurt as badly as Rachel had been. And, mixed up with the pain of her own loss, she felt a sudden savage anger towards Lorne Quentin.

Did he *have* to do this? Did he have to make that child fly out to Munich so that he could seduce her there? Couldn't he have been open about it all, approached Garfield honestly, especially when he must have known the tycoon would have wholeheartedly approved the engagement?

But Kelita didn't seem to believe that. She seemed to think that Garfield would object strenuously. She couldn't be blamed for wanting these few days, for wanting a romantic weekend before the shouting began.

Rachel sighed and turned to go back to the dining-room to wish Garfield goodbye. After their recent pact of friendship, she felt guilty at not telling him what his daughter was doing. But she'd made a promise, and anyway telling him now could only make the situation worse. Kelita was eighteen after all, and able to make up her own mind what to do with her life. It really wasn't any of Rachel's business.

Life was altogether too complicated, she thought sadly. Lorne, Garfield, Kelita, herself. They had become like balls of wool, inextricably tangled by some malicious kitten.

Maybe, she thought heavily, it was time to cut herself free.

Ten

By the following weekend, Rachel had done a lot of hard thinking. Faced with Lorne's betrayal, and hit by it even harder than by Graham's — and hadn't she known very well that she'd get hurt if she let herself get involved with Lorne Quentin? she asked herself savagely — she knew that there could no longer be a place for her at Quentin Motors. It wasn't that she had anything against Kelita — a long night's tussling with an uncomfortable honesty had proved to her that what she felt was simple jealousy, an emotion she had always prided herself on keeping under control. Even with Graham and Sue, she had managed to keep a sense of proportion as far as the other girl was concerned. *She* hadn't known Rachel was living with Graham. Neither had Kelita known that Rachel had fallen in love with Lorne. And the younger girl's transparent joy, her open excitement and happiness, would have been hard to destroy, even though Rachel had found them equally hard to bear. With all her artifices stripped away,

Kelita had shown herself to be an ordinary, vulnerable teenager. Rachel had caught a glimpse of that vulnerability once or twice before and she remembered hoping that Lorne wouldn't take advantage of it. And he hadn't — not if he were sincerely in love with the girl. Which seemed quite possible; after all, he'd spoken quite tenderly of her to Rachel, saying how sorry he felt for her lonely childhood, how it seemed in some ways to parallel his own. Rachel supposed that it was a mixture of compassion and protectiveness he felt for Garfield Holt's daughter. Together with a quite understandable physical desire.

Well, so be it. If only he hadn't wanted Rachel as well! If only he hadn't looked at her with those smoky eyes, called her his love, fanned her own desire to a white heat that still tormented her, that would never quite cease its smouldering . . .

That was why Rachel couldn't stay at Quentin Motors. That was why she had to get away — as far and as fast as she could. And certainly before he brought Kelita here as his bride.

Sunday morning dawned as clear and warm as every other day seemed to be in this extraordinary summer. Rachel woke late, her brain clear at last now that she had made her decision. She felt calmer now, slightly light-headed and empty as if she had just recovered from an illness. She slipped out of bed, looking down from her window at the garden, ablaze with old-fashioned roses. The tiny patch of lawn glittered with dew, inviting her to come down and bathe her toes in its coolness. Rachel smiled — why not? It was mid-summer, and didn't midsummer dew have some special magic? Pulling a short terry housecoat round her, she ran barefoot down the narrow staircase and let herself out into the garden.

The dew was deliciously cold to her feet, and she trod carefully across the grass, turning to see the footprints she had made. The whole world was still; only a few birds twittered, the days of the dawn chorus over as they hurried about to fetch food for hungry nestlings. In the field over the hedge she could see a few cows and hear their steady munching of the grass. The scene was utterly peaceful, and in the magic of the dawn Rachel wondered why she had let her emotions get so out of hand. Surely she could take some of this peace into her own heart, forget the problems and troubles that seemed to have beset her lately. Sex was nothing but a

287

matter of survival, after all, survival of the human race. It didn't have to ruin your life if you decided to opt out.

That, she decided now, was just what she was going to do. Opt out of the sex-race. Forget men and live for herself. Indulge herself a little. *Enjoy* life.

She stretched her arms up to the sky, lifting her face to the sun. There was plenty of happiness to be found, she told herself, without men. If she could just learn to believe it . . .

"And a very pretty sight it is too," said a deep, velvety voice behind her. "You didn't tell me you were a sun-worshipper, Rachel. Or is this the way dryads work out on summer mornings?"

"Lorne!" she breathed, and turned slowly.

He was standing very close, so that she was almost in his arms at once. His white shirt was unbuttoned at the neck, the sleeves rolled up to reveal tanned arms. He looked incredibly, unbearably attractive, and she felt her knees weaken with desire. But there was no answering desire in his eyes. They were as grey as slate, flinty with anger, and Rachel felt her trembling increase with fear.

"Lorne," she whispered again. "But but

you can't be here! You're in Munich — with Kelita."

His frown deepened. "In Munich with Kelita? What the hell are you talking about?" There was a grating savagery in his voice that she hadn't heard before. He reached out and grasped her arm, jerking her hard against him. Rachel was suddenly aware of her near-nakedness — no more than a wisp of a nightgown under the robe — and she gasped as she felt her soft breasts crush against his chest. "What crazy idea have you got into your head now?" He glowered down at her, then went on brusquely: "Never mind. I've come here straight from the airport to talk to you — I don't intend to be side-tracked. You're too elusive, Rachel, you know that? I've been trying to get in touch with you all week — where in hell have you been?"

"I was away with my parents last weekend," she retorted, trying to overcome the peculiar power that he still had to turn her bones to jelly. "Not that it's any business of yours! And since then I've been working — carrying out *your* instructions."

"And totally ignoring my messages," he added curtly. "Why didn't you ring me back when I asked you to?"

"In Munich? You must be joking. I

couldn't see any need to, that's why. Everything was under control. I don't object to making international calls when they're necessary, but not just to pass the time of day. Have you any idea what they cost? Besides, I didn't like the tone of the message you left with Julie — it was more like a royal command."

"It was a heartfelt plea, as it happens," he said quietly. "Only your own attitude of mind could have read it any other way. And that's what I want to know, Rachel — what happened to change you? On Friday afternoon you could have been mine. You very nearly were. And then, during the time it took me to make a telephone call, you changed completely. Couldn't get away fast enough." He let her go and paced around the tiny lawn, running strong fingers through his dark, shaggy hair. "Didn't you have any idea what it might do to me, you running out on me like that? Oh, at first I thought you really had some genuine appointment, something you couldn't break — though I couldn't imagine what, didn't even want to. The doubts started to creep in then. That Viking friend of yours — Ben Marshall — I thought it must be him you were in such a hurry to see. I thought you must be lovers — it seemed only too likely that day he came to the office." He came close again, looked down at her with haunted eyes. "I heard you talking about him staying with you at your cottage — you sounded so happy, so excited. I suppose I knew then . . ."

"Knew what?" Rachel breathed. The world was still as she waited for his answer.

"Knew that I loved you." His fingers were trembling now as he ran them again through his tousled hair. "I'd known all along — right from that very first day — that I *wanted* you. That was why I didn't appoint you straightaway. To me, you spelt danger, the kind of danger I'd avoided so far." His mouth twisted wryly. "The danger of committing myself. What I didn't realise that I was already committed — from the first moment when you walked in through my office door. And after a few days, I couldn't resist you any longer, you were like a magnet, drawing me to you. I knew there could be something for us, something real, and I had to give it a chance. That's why I came to see you at your flat and offered you the job. I just had to see you again."

He turned away, pacing across the lawn. "I could see you were attracted to me, too, but that was as far as it seemed to go. You put up barriers I couldn't break down — even when I lost control and kissed you, even though I could feel your response, you still managed to hold me at bay. You nearly drove me wild, you know that?" His grin was crooked and Rachel shook her head wordlessly. How could she never have guessed that his inner turmoil was as great as her own? "I came to the conclusion that the attraction you felt was no more than physical," he said in a low voice. "And that wouldn't do. I knew by then that an affair with you wouldn't be enough — it had to be all or nothing."

If only they could have read each other's minds, Rachel thought with numb despair. But what difference would it have made in the end? Lorne would still have betrayed her, and the pain would have been all the greater if they had loved each other first.

"And then Marshall arrived and I was sure," he went on. "That Friday — I believed that was why you rushed off so suddenly. Though if that were so I couldn't understand why you'd let *me* make love to you. Unless . . ." He took her by the arms, looking down into her face with searching eyes. "Unless you'd realised then that it was me you loved. I thought maybe you needed time to sort out your own feelings. I hoped that then . . .." Letting her go, he paced the lawn again, jerking at his hair so that it stood wildly on end. "God knows *what* I thought. And what with having to go and see Arthur, and then this trip to Munich . . .." He came close again and looked down at her, his eyes cloudy. "I was going to ask you to come with me to Munich, Rachel. I thought a few days away from the factory might help us to sort ourselves out. But you never answered your phone."

"I told you," she said dully. "I was in Devon." Would it have made any difference, she wondered, if she had gone to Munich with Lorne? There was still the matter of Ben's plans to be explained. Hadn't Lorne realised that she'd seen them, taken them?

"Rachel," Lorne said quietly, his voice deepened with an unmistakable sincerity. "You've got to tell me everything, *everything* that's been wrong between us. OK, maybe there's something we *can't* put right, but we don't have a chance if we don't talk honestly to each other. Let's give it a try anyway, shall we?"

Rachel stood quite still under his hands. She looked up into his face, searching for the truth. Yes, she would have staked her life that Lorne meant every word he said. But she'd been wrong before. Could she take the risk?

She thought of her determination, only moments before Lorne's arrival, to forget men — to forget this one in particular. That little resolution hadn't lasted five minutes. As soon as she saw him — as soon as he touched her — she was like putty in his hands. What chance had she of ever getting away?

Did she really want to get away?

"Think about it," Lorne said suddenly. "Sit down out here and think about it, while I make some coffee. You look exhausted, Rachel. And I don't mind telling you, I don't feel too bright myself." He guided her over to the garden seat and wiped the dew from it with his handkerchief. "Sit there and wait."

Rachel sat on the bench, listening to the soft sounds of the morning. A robin hopped out on to the lawn, followed by a fledgling as big as itself; Rachel watched while the parent bird tugged a worm from the grass and presented it to the baby. She heard the solitary chime of the village church bell, calling people to early service. A movement in the hedge attracted her attention and she watched while a hedgehog snuffled its way home after the night's foraging.

By the time Lorne returned, bearing a heaped plate of buttered toast as well as coffee, she had made up her mind.

"Eat and drink first," Lorne ordered, handing her a brimming mug. "We're going to need all our strength for this little session." His voice was humorous, and Rachel gave him a tentative smile. Somehow, she felt better already. There were still so many questions to which she didn't know the answers, but all at once she felt sure that there *were* answers — even if not the ones she'd envisaged.

"Lorne," she said when they'd finished the toast and were sitting close together with coffee-mugs warming their hands, "were you really not in Munich with Kelita?"

He turned and looked down at her, smiling that lazy, devastating smile that turned her heart over.

"I was not." He paused. "Believe me — or do you want details?"

Rachel wanted details. She wanted to know just why Kelita had given her the impression that she was spending the weekend with Lorne. But she waited a moment and thought about it. This was, she knew, an important moment. If Lorne and she were to make any kind of relationship — and she still didn't know what he had in mind — there had to be trust between them. Trust on both sides.

"I believe you," she said at last. "I don't want any details."

Lorne smiled and slipped his arm round her shoulders.

"You mean you do, but you're not going to ask," he teased. "Well, thank you for that, Rachel." His lips met hers in a brief kiss. "As it happens, there aren't any details to give. I went to Munich — alone. Stayed there — alone. Came back — alone. End of story. Why Kelita should tell you I was with her, I can't imagine, unless it was spite. But somehow she doesn't strike me as being a spiteful child — just rather young and confused at present. And I don't think she even knew I was going to Munich."

"You never told her?"

He shook his head. "I haven't seen her for weeks." His brows creased. "Rachel, why are you so worried about Kelita? How did she get between us? I've only met her two or three times at most the time when we went over to Garfield's together, at that appalling cocktail party she invited me to — and she was quite right, it was dreadful — and again one day when she came over to the factory in Garfield's place. That was the day your Ben came, remember? I was expecting Garfield and he couldn't come at the last minute, so Kelita brought some papers I needed and I was more or less forced to take her to lunch." His eyes darkened. "From the way you were behaving with Marshall, I should say *I* was the one who should worry."

Rachel shook her head. "Not for a moment. Ben and I are old friends, just as I told you, but there was never anything between us. And he's involved with another girl — a girl we both knew at college. But I wonder why Kelita —"

"Are you *sure* she said she was spending the weekend with me?" Lorne asked again. "I'd certainly like to know why, if she did. Think hard, Rachel — you couldn't possibly have misunderstood her?"

Rachel frowned, trying hard to remember. "I honestly *thought* she did. But maybe . . ." She went over every word Kelita had said — an easy enough procedure, for they'd been burning into her mind ever since. "No," she said slowly, "she didn't actually *say* she was going with

297

you. Just that she'd got engaged — she showed me the ring — and was going to the airport. I assumed it was to meet you because . . . because . . ." Her face cleared. "Of course! Because Garfield had been telling me how pleased he was that you and she looked like making a match of it! He didn't actually know for sure — I mean, Kelita hadn't told him definitely — but there was certainly a man 'in the off-ing' as he said, and he was convinced it must be you." Rachel looked up into Lorne's face. "The little minx," she said wonderingly. "She's been using your name to hide the fact that she's got a boyfriend Garfield wouldn't approve of! She *told* me she thought he'd hit the roof if he knew — and I thought she meant because you were so much older than she is. And all the time it was someone else!"

Lorne grinned. "I suppose I ought to be furious," he admitted. "But I can't help being rather amused. Garfield's got himself a handful there, but she's an attractive little monkey. All that sophistication was sheer pretence, you know. Underneath, she's as nervous as a kitten and as unsure of herself as a baby."

"You seem to know a great deal about her, for someone who's only met her three times," Rachel said demurely, and Lorne gave her cheek a playful flick with his finger.

"Enough of your impertinence, woman. And now — have you any other little issues you'd like to bring up before we proceed to the next item on the agenda?"

Rachel gave him a quick glance and decided not to ask what that might be. "Yes, there is one." She hesitated. This could be the trickiest question of all, and one that might not have such an easy solution as the issue of Kelita Holt. "Lorne, what were you doing with copies of Ben's plans in your room?"

"Copies of Ben's —" He stared at her, then comprehension dawned. "So *that's* what happened on Friday afternoon? You found them and thought I'd —" His eyes narrowed in disbelief, and Rachel nodded miserably. "You thought I was stealing his designs," Lorne finished incredulously.

"What else was I to think?" she asked unhappily. "You'd refused even to consider his plans. You'd turned them down. I remembered leaving them in your office and knew you must have copied them then, before I came to get them back. If that wasn't what you were doing, why *were* they there, Lorne?" She met his eyes, searching for the truth.

"They were there," he said slowly, looking at her intently, "because Ben Marshall sent them to me. Because after I'd turned them down — after we'd quarrelled — I thought again. I realised that I'd dismissed them so summarily, not because they weren't any good, but because I was downright jealous." He took a breath and said: "I realised that I was jealous because I loved you. But that was a separate issue. And it wasn't fair to take it out on Ben Marshall. Even less was it fair to take it out on a whole continent, who might well benefit from the designs I'd tossed aside out of petty spite."

Rachel gazed at him. It was an admission that couldn't have been easy to make — either to himself or to her. She knew then that she had wronged Lorne; that he was not a second Graham, that his actions would never be mean or petty, or anything less than honest.

"I contacted Marshall and asked him to let me have the plans again," Lorne went on quietly. "They'd arrived that day and I'd been looking at them in the morning. With all the excitement of Arthur's party and illness, and then my trip to Munich — not to mention the turmoil I was in over you, my sweet — I didn't have time to give them any further attention. I was going to sit down and go over them this week — with your help, if you'd give it. There are quite a few ideas I've got that could make them a viable proposition, and like you I think it would be a rewarding thing to do."

"You mean you're going to go ahead with it? You'll build the Indian T?"

He nodded. "I want to talk it over with Ben, of course. And you, Rachel — I want you in on the discussions. You've proved with the new executive people-carrier that you've got a firm grasp of the practical side of using a car. I don't know if I've ever told you how pleased Garfield is with what we've come up with." Rachel hid a smile. "But that car's going to be a winner, without compromising the Quentin style one iota. And it's more than cleared the economic situation for us. Which means that we can afford to give a bit. And I can't think of anything better than Ben's car to give to the Third World."

"It's just the design," Rachel said eagerly. "And making a few protypes — we won't be producing them for ever, there's no ongoing line to think about."

"I know. It's all right, Rachel — you're preaching to the converted." He grinned.

"It's going to be an exciting project. And we're going to be working on it together. I'm looking forward to it."

"So that's everything cleared up," Rachel said after a moment.

"Everything — except why young Kelita's been taking my name in vain, and what her father's going to do when he finds out. Which is really their problem, not ours at all, and probably not so very terrible anyway. Maybe we could take the child under our wing a little. She seems to like me, and if she's told you she's engaged she must like you too." Lorne's eyes glinted down at her. "And Garfield certainly will find out, my darling, when he hears that *we're* engaged. We are, aren't we?" he added with a sudden anxiety that made Rachel laugh.

"Well, you haven't asked me to marry you," she said demurely, "but I suppose you could quite easily put that right . . . Oh, Lorne!" her voice shook as he kissed her with lips that were meant to be tender but quickened with the depth of their feelings to become a kiss of heart-shaking passion. "Lorne, I love you so much. I've been in such a muddle." Soon she would tell him all about Graham. But it wasn't the time now for any further confessions, she

302

decided as Lorne drew her closer against him. "Let's not talk any more," she whispered against those searching lips. "Let's just be together."

His fingers shook slightly as he parted the neck of her robe and touched her breast. She felt the now familiar fire spread from his touch, enveloping her body with its warmth, and lay back in his arms, neck arched for his kisses. Her hands wandered up to his hair, tangling in its thick dark waves, holding his head close against her.

"We'll be together," he muttered hoarsely. "Together for the rest of our lives. And that's a promise."

They sat very close on the garden bench, watching the robin, the bees on the roses, the small movements of other garden birds in the hedge. Rachel told Lorne about the hedgehog.

"He's gone to bed now," she remarked, and felt Lorne's lips brush her cheek.

"Perhaps we should follow his example," he murmured, and with a smile she got up and led him indoors.